The torment **belief.**

"You don't know what you're risking."

"I have nothing more to risk, Ivan."

His head tilted back against her hand, a growl rumbling deep in his chest. He was resisting because he *did* fear he'd hurt her.

Anastasia had to make him believe her that he wouldn't, had to make him stop holding back. Her other hand slipped around his neck, coaxing his face down to hers, needing to snap his hesitation. "The only injury I could have sustained was letting you go without being with you one more time."

Moving closer, she lowered her arms to hug all she could of him, a breath she'd been holding for seven years flowing out in tortured relief. Until he stiffened in her embrace.

Before she could withdraw in mortification, his formidable body surrendered.

Then suddenly he was pushing away and she was off her feet and in his arms.

* * *

His Pregnant Christmas Bride is part of
The Billionaires of Black Castle series—

Only their dark pasts could lead these men
to the light of true love.

Dear Reader,

Since I started writing The Billionaires of Black Castle series, Ivan Konstantinov insisted on telling me very little about himself. That only made me even more anxious to learn his story.

Then, suddenly, in Antonio Balducci's book, *Billionaire Boss, M.D.*, Ivan explosively interrupted a huge emotional turning point, making me unable to wait to know his story.

And what a heart-wrenching story it was. I do believe it's the most emotional one of all the brothers'. No wonder, really, since Ivan was the one who came to The Organization old enough to know his family. He was the one with enough tech skills to never lose sight of them, but was the only one who never tried to seek that family once he was free. And I just knew there had to be a devastating reason why. Sure enough, it was even more so than I imagined.

I really hope you enjoy Ivan and Anastasia's story as much as I enjoyed writing it!

I love to hear from readers, so please visit my website, www.oliviagates.com, or email me at oliviagates@gmail.com. You can also connect with me on Facebook, www.Facebook.com/oliviagatesauthor, on Goodreads, www.Goodreads.com/author/show/405461.olivia_gates, and on Twitter, @oliviagates.

Thanks for reading!

Olivia Gates

OLIVIA GATES

———

HIS PREGNANT CHRISTMAS BRIDE

ISBN-13: 978-0-373-73496-2

His Pregnant Christmas Bride

Copyright © 2016 by Olivia Gates

This edition published by arrangement with Harlequin Books S.A.

For questions and comments about the quality of this book, please contact us at CustomerService@Harlequin.com.

® and TM are trademarks of Harlequin Enterprises Limited or its corporate affiliates. Trademarks indicated with ® are registered in the United States Patent and Trademark Office, the Canadian Intellectual Property Office and in other countries.

Printed in U.S.A.

HARLEQUIN®
www.Harlequin.com

USA TODAY bestselling author **Olivia Gates** has written over forty books in action/adventure, thriller, medical, paranormal and contemporary romance. Her signature is her über-alpha male heroes. Whether they're gods, black-ops agents, virtuoso surgeons or ruthless billionaires, they all fall in love once and for life with the only women who can match them and bring them to their knees. She loves to hear from readers, so don't hesitate to email her at oliviagates@gmail.com.

Visit the Author Profile page at Harlequin.com, or oliviagates.com, for more titles.

One

The beeping of the instruments measuring Anastasia Shepherd's vitals quickened as she surfaced from her oppressive slumber.

But she didn't want to wake up. She preferred the horrors she faced in sleep over the nightmare her life had become after the attack that had ended her brother's life, and left her struggling for hers.

She squeezed her lids harder against the macabre images. The masked gunmen, the muted gunfire, the crimson blossoming over Alex's white shirt as he collapsed beside her, bullets tearing into her own body.

In her shock, she'd somehow known she wouldn't die, not immediately. She'd also known one other thing. That she'd needed to protect her brother from further injury with whatever was left of her life. She'd thrown herself over Alex's body as their attackers approached them like inescapable doom.

But she'd only seen them fall. Like disposable opponents in a vicious video game at the hands of an expert player. It had made no sense. Until she'd seen *him*.

Ivan.

The man who'd walked away from her without a word seven years ago.

He'd swooped down on her and Alex, and right before darkness had claimed her, she'd heard him say what she'd dreamed he'd come back one day and say.

I'm here now.

And he'd been with her ever since. Through the whole ordeal of the past three weeks. Always sitting beside her bed like a sentinel. Watching over her, catering to her every need. Answering none of her questions.

"It isn't a mercy anymore, Ivan."

The words she hadn't intended to voice just came out, laden with all her agony and frustration, before she even opened her eyes.

Ivan made no response, probably thinking she was talking in her sleep. But she felt him move closer, until he was standing over her.

She finally forced her eyes open and was once again overwhelmed by his sheer beauty and physical presence.

He'd always been the most incredible man she'd ever seen. The exact combination that had appealed to her every taste and enslaved her every sense. In the short time she'd known him, she hadn't been able to tear her eyes and thoughts off of him. Not to mention her hands, lips and every inch of her. No man had ever compared to him, before or since; she'd given up before she'd even tried.

But the thirty-three-year-old juggernaut she'd once known had been nothing compared to the forty-year-old god he'd become.

Everything about him had been…magnified, intensified, until it choked her up just looking at him, just feeling him near. Any softness she hadn't even realized he'd had had been chiseled away. What remained looked as if it had been carved from polished steel, perfect and impenetrable.

If she didn't feel like one raw, exposed nerve, she knew she would have found him even more attractive for it. But how could she possibly be more attracted to him now than she had been in the past? From that first glance, when her brother introduced him as a new friend and another expatriate from their motherland, Russia, she'd been helplessly drawn to him like iron filings were to a magnet.

"Anastasia, are you awake?"

It seemed he wasn't sure, even with her eyes open and locked on his. She must have sleep-talked too many times.

She answered him by pressing the bed's remote, bringing herself up to a reclining position. "Avoiding my questions, giving me no details or explanations, is only making it worse."

When she'd thought nothing could make the devastation of losing Alex so violently any worse.

Her brother, her mentor and champion and closest friend, was gone. *Murdered.* That she'd survived was irrelevant. Unfair. If one of them had to die, it should have been her. Alex was far more important, in so many ways, to so many more people.

But not knowing why or who had been responsible for this heinous crime ate away at her sanity.

Ivan had only told her that he'd snatched her and Alex from the scene before law enforcement or emergency services had arrived, had provided them with lightning-fast medical stabilization while transporting them to his partner, Antonio Balducci, the only doctor he could trust with their lives.

She'd known Ivan and his partners in Black Castle Enterprises were extremely rich and powerful, but this level of reach and resources was mind-boggling. Ivan had been able to intervene faster than the authorities, who clearly hadn't even been alerted, since nobody had come investigating the attack. While this state-of-the-art hospital that far surpassed any medical facility she'd ever heard about was off-the-map. That something of that caliber was unknown to the world spoke of unimaginable power.

But though Dr. Balducci's fame had reached even her in the nonmedical world, as a genius trauma surgeon whose work bordered on magic, he'd managed to save only her.

Dr. Balducci had told her Ivan's intervention had given them a shot at surviving when nothing else could have. But only she had been in any condition to do so, even with his unequaled skills. There had been no saving Alex.

And she still didn't understand *why*. Any of it. The attack, Ivan's reappearance, anything he'd done ever since. Each time she inquired, Ivan merely insisted she wasn't strong enough yet to worry about anything but recuperating. He wouldn't tell her a thing.

He'd been the only man she'd ever loved, and he'd streaked in and out of her life like a meteor, leaving only wreckage in his wake. For him to be back in her life in such an explosive, inexplicable way had at first paralyzed her ability to think. Now speculation and confusion were driving her insane.

"Just tell me everything. *Please*."

His solicitous gaze became a stormy sea-green in the warmly lit hospital suite, as he clearly struggled with his reluctance to do so. Then his massive chest finally expanded on a resigned inhalation.

"I only wanted you to recuperate without having to deal with distressing details. I also wanted to…resolve the situation before I told you everything." He lowered his head for a moment before he looked up at her again. "I'm sorry if I inadvertently added to your anguish. That was the last thing I wanted to do."

Had he also thought he'd been sparing her when he'd left her seven years ago? Had he been trying not to "add to her anguish" by leaving without a word or warning?

Now that she thought about it, probably. He'd always felt somewhat…detached from the rest of humanity. Now he seemed to be wholly so. He probably had no insight into how he made others feel, how his actions impacted them. It stood to reason he didn't realize that he'd almost destroyed her by his sudden and unexplained desertion in the past—and was as equally clueless how his actions affected her now.

Not that she could be bitter about his actions this time. He had saved her. Had been dedicated to her physical well-being. He was merely oblivious to the rest of her needs, emotional and psychological. Like he'd always been.

Raising the bed to a fully sitting position, she vaguely noted that the surgical wound across her abdomen where Dr. Balducci had put her back together barely pulled. It now caused her minimum discomfort, even with reduced pain medication.

"I'm sorry, too, Ivan. The last thing I want is to seem ungrateful after everything you've been doing for me. I'm more grateful than I can say. But I not only can handle the full truth now, I need it. Nothing could be worse than what already happened, and the only way I can deal with it is to make sense of it all."

That seemed to flabbergast him. She'd been right. He'd never even considered this could be how she'd be feeling.

When he finally nodded, his hands fisted at his sides. Hands that had once owned her body in total intimacy. But that had been in another life. In this new realm, he hadn't once touched her since he'd squeezed her hand as he'd told her of Alex's death.

"I'll tell you everything you want to know," he said,

looking like he'd rather take a bullet himself than do so. "But I need you to promise something first." She nodded, wary at the flare in his eyes. "Never apologize for anything. Or feel grateful. Never to me."

It really seemed to offend him, even pain him, that she'd expressed her regret and gratitude.

Would she ever understand the enigma that was Ivan Konstantinov?

No. It didn't matter that she never would. This wasn't about him, or about them. This was about Alex. She had to know why he'd been murdered, how she could avenge him.

Once he had her conceding nod, he exhaled forcibly. "You were attacked because of Alex's discoveries and intentions."

Ivan waited a beat, no doubt to see her response. She had none.

He grimaced. "I know about the top-secret, alternative energy project Alex was helming for FuturEn in conjunction with the multinational International Energy Organization, and that you were taking part as one of his top physicists. No need to pretend you don't know what I'm talking about."

She shook her head dazedly. "I'm not pretending anything." He looked as if he'd cut her off, but she hurried to add, "It doesn't surprise me that you know this. Now that I have a better idea of the extent of your power, it would surprise me if you didn't know everything about everyone who's ever crossed your path. What I don't understand is why Alex would be targeted for assassination for his work. It isn't as if he's the first person to ever make a breakthrough in such a field."

"You really don't know, do you?" When she shook her head, his teeth made a terrible grinding sound. He clearly hated that he had to explain more than he'd bargained for. "I expected as his research partner and sister, he'd confided in you that he'd discovered tampering at the highest levels in both the private research facility and the IEA to falsify his results."

The revelation hit her like a punch to her tender gut.

She slumped back, the ever-hovering tears flowing down her cheeks again.

Ivan stabbed a hand in his raven mane, his frown one of realization. "He must have wanted to shield you from it all, must have wanted to expose the fraud without your involvement to protect you. Yet it's clear he didn't think they'd decide to silence him forever."

A sob tore through her even as she struggled to bring herself under control. "H-how did you find all that out when I didn't even suspect any of it?"

The reluctance to give her information about himself, what had always been his default, tightened his face further. "I have my ways, Anastasia."

Yeah. That he had. Being called the king of the cyber world must mean he had an ear and an eye, not to mention a hand, in just about everything that made the world go round.

"But if you found out the liquidation plan, why didn't you warn Alex? Or…did you warn him and he didn't believe it would come to that?"

"Alex was very careful in covering his tracks as he investigated the culprits and gathered evidence against them. So careful even I didn't trace it until he requested an emergency meeting with all key players in the project, no doubt to make his revelation. It was just a couple of hours before the meeting when I pieced together the whole thing."

She bit her trembling lip. "The meeting he told me he'd go to alone."

"He wanted you away from any possible fallout, which he probably thought would only involve professional setbacks or legal repercussions. It's clear he didn't realize how huge this was to those he was going to expose. He didn't imagine they'd kill to stop him." His jaw muscles bunched and those emerald eyes grew more turbid. "In the tight time I had, I had two options: alerting the police with an unsubstantiated claim, and only having them protect Alex temporarily if they even moved in time. Or I had to intervene myself, as the one equipped to effect comprehensive and permanent protection. I tried to call Alex to tell him to stay put until I came to extract him. I sent him messages, to no avail. And though I suspected you wouldn't be with him, I tried you, too. I had no response from you, either."

"He—he always forgot to take his phone off Mute. I keep mine on Vibrate, but I hadn't even looked at my phone that morning. I—I was too focused on getting to him before he left for that meeting."

"I almost went out of my mind being unable to reach either of you so I could warn you."

"But how did you get to us in time?" This she had to know.

His grimness deepened. "I didn't get to you in time."

"You almost did…"

"Almost doesn't count. I couldn't save Alex."

She swallowed another red-hot shard of agony at the reminder. "What I mean is, how were you so close that you reached us so quickly?"

"My Black Castle headquarters, with my apartment above it, is half an hour's drive from your labs. I came by helicopter."

He'd been that close? She'd spent the past years thinking he'd returned to Russia, or was flitting around the world, never settling in one place like he'd once said he never would. Had he been that close all along? So near she could have stumbled upon him on the streets?

Maybe she had. Maybe it was why she'd always felt him around her. Maybe he'd crossed her path many times but had remained out of sight.

He went on. "On the way, I saw the GPS signals of your phones next to each other. My blood froze when I realized you were together when you've been working in different labs during this phase of the research."

She nodded, stunned yet again at the extent of his knowledge of her and Alex's routines and the latest developments in their research, not to mention his ability to track them with such pinpoint accuracy. "I had a feeling Alex wasn't telling me something important about that emergency meeting so I went to him instead of going to my lab. To see if I could persuade him to let me join him."

His nod was terse, bleak. "The moment I realized you were together, I knew it would be the perfect time for them to strike. I knew they'd assume what I did, that he'd taken you into his confidence and you had to be eliminated with him. I have no doubt they would have leveled the whole building to destroy all evidence had I not arrived when I had."

The memories assaulted her, vivid and palpable. She choked as she felt as if she'd been thrown back into the horrifying moments all over again. "I'd just walked into his lab…and before I could say anything to him, they—they…"

Horror and agony filled her throat again, sealing it, cutting off her words, her breath. But she had to ask, had to know.

"I—I saw our attackers fall. Did you…?"

Ivan again looked as scary as he had during those moments when he'd swooped down on her and Alex. "I took care of them."

"You k-killed them?"

Her answer was a terrifying flare in his eyes. Not only affirming that he had, but also telling her he wanted nothing more than to resurrect them so he could have the pleasure of killing them over and over, this time slowly, agonizingly.

This was an Ivan she hadn't known, hadn't dreamed existed. Not the virtuoso cyber entrepreneur or the dream lover. This was a seasoned warrior, a remorseless exterminator. It made her wonder again if she'd ever truly known him.

Not that seeing this lethal side to him upset or scared her. It didn't even occur to her to be bothered about the illegality of his actions. He'd exacted immediate revenge that she considered just. Had she been able to, she would have done the same.

The need to know what else he'd done burned her. "What else did you do? Besides get us here?"

"I erased every sign of the attack."

"You removed the bodies?"

His nod was so matter-of-fact it made her wonder how many times he'd been involved in situations like this. It seemed this man she was discovering she knew very little about had dealt with lethal scenarios so many times before, he'd developed an unblinking ability to take ruthless action and had all the resources in place to resolve any problem. She'd only heard about such power and abilities in spy and black ops thrillers. So who exactly was Ivan Konstantinov?

She prodded him for more details. "What did you do with them?"

Ferociousness simmered again in his eyes. "No need to concern yourself with them, ever again. No one will ever find them. Along with the evidence of what they did to you and Alex." At her confused expression he continued. "To your colleagues and employers, Alex had to cancel the meeting as both he and you had to leave on emergency family business. To your families, you're on sensitive, confidential work-related business that necessitated you leave immediately and remain out of contact until it's over. I send them messages from both your phones regularly to reassure them."

So he'd really covered every angle. Still, her breath came out in painful spurts as she imagined their families. Three weeks had passed since their abrupt disappearance. "They must still be going mad with worry."

His frown darkened. "I know. I try my best to placate them but I can only postpone their devastation, as this served many purposes."

Unable to contain her frustration anymore, she seethed. "What purposes? Why won't you let me contact them? Why don't you want the police involved even now? What—"

He cut off her agitated questions, his voice and gaze soothing, compelling. "Because I needed to keep the assassins' masters in the dark about what happened until I dealt with them all."

"That's why you didn't take us to a regular hospital and had Dr. Balducci take charge of us there?"

His eyes flooded with what looked like relief, that she'd reached that conclusion. "I couldn't even take you to one of his publicly known medical facilities where you could have been seen and recognized. I had to make sure those involved in the crime would never pose danger to you or anyone of yours, or anyone at all, ever again." At the fresh surge of tears in her eyes, he gritted his teeth again. "I know now I should have told you more of this sooner. But I still wouldn't have let you contact your family. It would have placed them in danger if they'd learned any of it before I concluded everything."

"And did you? Conclude everything?"

"I'm putting the finishing touches on it all today."

This probably meant far worse than she, in her previously oblivious life, could imagine. Even now, she couldn't speculate on what he was doing. But after finding out the truth of the big picture, she no longer wanted to know the details.

But one thing she did know—Ivan was unstoppable. Whatever it took to end this with no more damage or danger to her or any of Alex's loved ones, he would do it. He'd already done it, was just wrapping up the loose ends now.

And no matter what he'd said, she was grateful, with all the ferocity of the agony and rage that were the only things fueling her will to live now.

He stood straighter, his eyes taking on a solemn cast. "Now you know. But there's one thing more I need you to understand. You have nothing to fear anymore, Anastasia. Never again. I pledge it."

His vow, along with the ramifications of his revelations, sank deep in her mind, drying her tears, stifling her agitation. She stared up at his hard, arresting face, and felt even more confusion and questions swamping her.

Years ago he'd been her lover, the embodiment of all her fantasies, the sum total of everything she could have never dreamed of. Then one day it was over. He'd said he was traveling on business. Then he'd never contacted her again.

The end had been so sudden she would have believed something terrible had happened to him if she hadn't read about him in media sources that covered the rich and famous. It had forced her to stop her efforts to contact him after one unanswered try. For only one thing could explain his ending it like that. In their incendiary, if short-lived affair, all the passion and emotion had only been on her side.

Yet everything he'd been doing since the attack contradicted that assumption. None of that was the actions of a man who cared nothing for her, or for Alex, whom he'd cut off as well. Everything he'd told her proved he'd kept close tabs on her. He'd come to their rescue without a moment's hesitation, and he continued to go to unimaginable lengths to eliminate any further danger to her and her family, and to avenge Alex. He'd been unwaveringly there for her through this ordeal, by her side from the moment he'd rescued her.

It was beyond confusing. But she was also beyond attempting to make sense of it all.

She could do nothing but let him steer the situation as he saw fit. He had all the knowledge, and all the power, while she was demolished, fragile in body and psyche.

She nodded weakly, accepting his vow and admitting her need for his protection, then lowered her aching, trembling body back to a supine position.

"I know you don't want thanks, Ivan, but you have mine. I'd do anything to repay you." His growl started to interrupt her but she closed her eyes, aborting his exasperation. Before she let exhaustion drag her into nothingness again, she whispered one last thing. "Let me know when you decide it's safe to contact our families."

Ivan watched Anastasia's breathing even out until it was the imperceptible movements that had at first sent him berserk, thinking it was a sign of deterioration.

But he'd been finding other things to compromise his sanity—her gemlike azure eyes, which had turned muddy, her peaches-and-cream complexion and even her long, thousand-hues golden hair that had become ashen, and her body, which had lost its lush curves and looked more fragile by the day.

But Antonio had kept assuring him she was getting better, and he'd been by her side day and night making sure she continued to do so, watching for every sliver of improvement.

Now the last words she'd said before she'd slipped back into oblivion reverberated in his head.

Our families.

She'd meant her and Alex's families: their parents, Alex's wife and children, and his in-laws, who were like a second family to both of them.

She couldn't know one of those families was his, too.

Keeping that fact a secret, keeping away from that family, had been one of the two reasons he'd forced himself to walk away from her and Alex years ago. Though he'd told her a lot today, that was one revelation he was keeping to himself. As it was, what he'd revealed of the tragedy had hit her hard enough.

But she'd made him tell her. And soon the need to keep their families in the dark would be over and her family's grief would only add to hers.

Dealing with the scum responsible for Alex's murder had been the easy part of this disaster. The hard part—and what kept getting harder—was dealing with everything that concerned Anastasia. His dread for her. His inability to give her her life back, with her body intact and her brother alive. And the expectation that he'd soon have to relinquish her again.

But the hardest thing of all was her very nearness.

When he'd deprived himself of it seven years ago, he'd thought he'd eventually become numb to the loss. It had taken one look into her eyes, in those nightmarish moments when he'd thought he'd been too late to save her, to prove how wrong he had been.

He hadn't been numb; he'd been shut down completely. It had been the only way to continue functioning. The injury of her loss, what he'd inflicted on himself, agonized and hardened him like none of the ordeals of his hellish past had. And that had been when she'd been alive and well. In the time he'd thought she might die, too, he'd known he wouldn't survive losing her for real.

But he hadn't lost her. Antonio had saved her.

At first he'd hidden Alex's fate from her, and the details of what he'd done, in order to hide his true nature. Anastasia and Alex had known him as Ivan Konstantinov, not Wildcard, The Organization's lethal mercenary with a body count that neither of them could have thought existed except in fictional tales or real-life stories of monsters.

But she'd insisted on seeing Alex until he had to tell her the truth. Watching her almost disintegrate with grief, he'd been grateful he hadn't told her she'd only survived because of the liver transplant she'd gotten from Alex.

As it had turned out, he should have told her, not about the transplant, but about the rest. Now that she was privy to everything, she was letting him deal with everything as he saw fit. He should have trusted her then to make the rational decision. After all, the Anastasia he knew never let emotions interfere with pragmatic priorities.

When he'd walked away, she'd only tried to contact him once. When he'd made no response, she'd gone on with her life as if those magical weeks they'd shared hadn't happened.

At first, instead of being relieved that his desertion hadn't hurt her, that she'd decided to just move on, he'd hated it, had felt such contrary bitterness that had made him even more ruthless and cynical.

But he'd still been unable to stop watching her and Alex obsessively. And as time had gone by and she'd been too busy with her scientific studies and research career to move on, he'd felt perverse pleasure that she hadn't replaced him. Even if she had, he still would have helped her. And he had, opening doors for her and Alex that would have remained closed otherwise. Their success had been deserved, but even in the world of science, it wasn't always merit that saw someone get their dues. He'd seen to it that they did.

It had remained a struggle to keep away even when he'd believed her better off without him. He lived in fear his past would catch up with him and he'd place her and Alex in danger. That had been the main reason he'd walked away.

It was such tragic irony that when fatal danger had targeted her and Alex, it had had nothing to do with him.

His phone buzzed in his pocket. Getting it out before the noise could wake her, he read the message he'd been waiting for. Fyodor, his right hand, affirming his latest move had been carried out.

Alex's murderers had been neutralized.

There was no reason to put off contacting Anastasia's and Alex's families anymore.

Not that his reluctance had anything to do with caring what *they* would suffer once they knew the truth. If not for them being Alex's family, if it wasn't for them continuing to impact Anastasia's life, he wouldn't have considered them at all.

After all, they were the people who'd sent him to hell.

Two

"Don't discharge her."

Ivan blocked Antonio's path in the deserted corridor, intercepting him on the way to Anastasia's room.

His best friend's turbid eyes clashed with his unwaveringly, in their depths things Ivan had never seen before. Not even during their worst days as The Organization's captives and mercenaries.

Antonio had always been their brotherhood's most sangfroid member, at times seeming inhuman in his ability to deal with any level of hardship or abuse with a level head and a cool smile. Even as his closest friend from childhood, who'd seen deeper into him than anyone else ever had, he'd never thought Antonio could feel like this, let alone be unable to hide it. Despondent, desperate, even a little unhinged.

But then what had seemed impossible had happened. Antonio had fallen in love. Violently, irrevocably. And Liliana, the woman who'd created a heart inside him to worship her with—in his friend's own words—had discovered the truth. That he'd started their relationship as a plot to infiltrate their joint family, to destroy them from within. Liliana now believed he'd never loved her, had only proposed as means to an end. Devastated at the discovery, she'd run away from his efforts to explain…and she'd almost been fatally injured in doing so. After spiraling through ten different kinds of hell as he'd operated on her, too, he'd saved her life. But clearly, not her love. Liliana's rejection seemed final.

Now Antonio, the surgeon with nerves of steel, was a total mess. Which could actually work to Ivan's advantage right now.

The old Antonio, whose emotions never played a role in his actions and decisions, would have turned down his demand, since there was no medical merit to it. But Antonio the emotional volcano might sympathize with his plight and do what Ivan wanted.

And what he wanted was to postpone Anastasia rejoining the world, and her family.

Shaking his head, Antonio said, "I have already kept her longer than necessary, to be on the safest side possible. There's now no medical reason not to let her go back to her life."

A shiver ran down Ivan's spine. Antonio's voice now was the scariest thing he'd ever heard. Such barely contained instability from the most controlled being he'd ever known.

He only hoped dragging Antonio into his own concerns would distract him from dwelling on his regrets and the loss of the woman who'd become his only reason for living.

"Listen, Tonio, I'm eternally grateful for what you've done for…Anastasia." It was still hard to say her name, even to Antonio. He hadn't told him a thing about her until she'd realized her surgeon didn't even know her name and provided him with it. "I'm thankful that she has healed enough for you to think she should be discharged—" He grabbed Antonio's arm when he turned away. "But I'm still demanding you don't do it."

Irritation flickered in Antonio's eyes at Ivan's detainment. "And you're not going to give me a reason for your demand?"

Ivan's fingers dug harder into Antonio's steel arm in frustration. "My asking it should be reason enough for you."

Antonio finally took exception to Ivan's effort to coerce him, prying his hand off his arm with equal vehemence. "It was when you were asking me to help her. I didn't need to know anything then. I was willing to wait forever for you to tell me why she and her brother were shot or who they are to you. But now you're asking me to lie to her, to keep her here against her will."

"Who says it would be against her will?"

"She does. She wants to leave."

"She wants no such thing. And she certainly said nothing to you. I was there every second you were with her."

A ghost of the teasing they'd always engaged in from childhood came into Antonio's gaze. "Yeah, that you were. But I let you sit in during my checkups only as a courtesy to you as my best friend, against my professional and better judgment." Any hint of that indulgence vanished, and he started moving past him. "So don't push your luck, Ivan."

Ivan grabbed both his arms this time. He wasn't letting him walk away. "I'm pushing more than that, Tonio. You might think she's ready to leave based on her physical condition, but I know what's best for her."

Antonio gave the hands digging into his flesh a disdainful look. "It's clear your need to keep her here is blinding you to *her* needs. But *I* feel her need to leave."

"You might be an unequaled genius, Tonio, but not even you are omniscient. Hell, you didn't even suspect what your own lover would feel if she knew the truth."

The moment the words were out, Ivan could have happily cut off his own tongue. The surge of self-loathing that came into Antonio's eyes would remain one of his stupidest, cruelest mistakes.

Ivan dropped his hands to his side, exhaled heavily. "I didn't mean it the way it sounded."

Antonio waved his qualification away. "I did know how she'd feel and that's why I hid the truth. *That* was my mistake."

"*I'm* not making one. She needs to stay here longer."

"If you think so, then you're having a serious judgment malfunction. She may not have asked to be discharged, but I sense she can't wait to bolt from here." Before Ivan could flay him with another contradiction, Antonio folded his arms over his white-coated chest. "Let me remind you that your specialty is ending lives, not saving them like me. Including yours, many times as I recall. So I'm the expert here."

"Not where Anastasia is concerned."

"Actually, in her case, your verdict is even more suspect, since you're clearly what I thought was impossible—emotionally involved. Even if it's in a way I can't fathom. It makes you even more ineligible to make decisions on her behalf."

Ivan felt his frustration rising to a suffocating level as his friend's eyes emptied of all agitation and became ice-cold blue.

Great. In his attempt at taking Antonio's mind off his estranged lover, he'd only brought out the immovable surgeon in him. To his own detriment.

He exhaled, pissed off at himself, at Antonio and all of existence. "Is this your roundabout way of forcing me to tell you about my involvement with her? You think you've found the best leverage to satisfy your curiosity?"

Antonio gave a disgusted shrug. "Right now I couldn't care less if the whole world, including you, disappeared, ended or even went to hell. But the one thing still functioning about me is my surgeon side." Yeah, like Ivan had just thought. "Professionally, I am obliged to tell her she's well enough to go. After that, she can choose to stay longer, or you convince her to stay. But I will tell her the truth. I won't let you hold her hostage to your own ends and convictions." Ivan started to protest, but Antonio raised a hand in a gesture of finality. "Either you give me a good enough reason not to discharge her, Ivan, or get out of my way."

So this was it. The only way Antonio would budge now was if Ivan played his last card. Much as he hated it, he had to tell him everything.

"Fine, I'll give you the reason." Feeling as if he was about to jump off a cliff, he inhaled a bolstering breath. "Got something stronger than coffee around here?"

Antonio turned away and started walking back toward his office. "I have medical-grade alcohol."

He fell into step with him. "Yeah, I forgot for a second there that you don't drink."

"Even if I did, I wouldn't keep my vices around my place of work."

"Yeah, well, for me to finally tell you what happened in my life before we met, we'll probably both need something."

"I have intravenous morphine." Antonio walked through his door, left Ivan to close it behind them. "Though I probably need sodium pentothal if I want anything approaching the truth. The maximum dose, for an elephant. You're the most drug-resistant ogre I've ever encountered."

Ivan threw himself on the black leather couch while

Antonio sat in his preferred armchair. "Still harping on when you wasted three times the dosage of anesthetic to put me under when you had to pull the shrapnel out of my thigh? I'd told you to do it with me awake. You're the one who wouldn't listen."

"I'll listen now." Antonio leaned forward and reached for the carafe on the table, poured one cup of black coffee. Ivan knew it was for him when Antonio added three spoons of sugar, as he knew he took it.

Grumbling that it was a poor substitute for Scotch, he took the cup from Antonio, at once taking a gulp, letting its contents scorch his throat.

Antonio sat back, leveled his gaze on him dispassionately. "So are you going to talk, or are you again going to be the elusive son of a bitch who never told even me anything about your past?"

Ivan snorted. "As if you were any better. You found out everything about your family and kept it to yourself, hatched this moronic vengeance plot that is now costing you the love of your life. If you'd told me, I would have probably saved you from making that catastrophic mistake."

"Yeah, sure. You would have saved me from myself."

"As I recall, I did, on a few notable, potentially fatal, incidents."

Antonio's frown took on a defensive edge. "I didn't want to share specifics until I felt I had something worthwhile to share. Besides, it's different. I didn't spend the last thirty years hiding the truth about my past from you. I didn't know anything about it until recently. But you came to The Organization old enough to know everything about yours."

"Touché." Ivan's grunt acknowledged the inequality of their positions. He'd always felt Antonio didn't like that he kept him, of all people, in the dark. But he'd never pushed.

He was pushing now. And maybe it was just as well. Maybe he needed to purge the poison bottled up in his system. And who better to help him do it but his best friend and the world's leading healer?

When he didn't start talking at once, Antonio started to rise. "Seems you do need a shot of sodium pentothal to help loosen that calcified tongue of yours."

Ivan barked a mirthless laugh at his friend's threat and gestured for him to settle down. "I'll talk without a truth serum. But when I do, you'll end up doing what I demanded. So maybe you should just save yourself listening to the heap of crap that is my life story and just do as I say."

Antonio sat back, waving nonchalantly. "What's new? I've been taking your crap since I was eleven. Talk already. But whatever you say, there's no guarantee it'll change my mind."

"Oh, it will."

"*No* guarantee."

"All right, fine. Here goes, then." At Antonio's encouraging nod, he felt he got a glimpse of his oldest and closest friend again. It made it easier to start. "I was born Konstantin Ivanovich in Russia before the collapse of the Soviet Union." He paused as under-

standing flared in Antonio's eyes. Every member of
their brotherhood had explained why he'd adopted his
current name, except Ivan. "Yes, that's why I chose
my name. Very predictable." He inhaled, went on.
"During the upheaval leading to the collapse, my
father found himself in a dangerous position. He'd
inherited his job as a bookkeeper in Russia's orga-
nized crime and he needed out—out of the mob,
and of the country. There was one great opportunity
where he could take our family to the United States,
and it all depended on me.

"I was only twelve, but I had long been recognized as a prodigy of computer programming. My
abilities had meant a lot to my father's bosses. But he
said there was this international organization offering children of exceptional abilities a unique opportunity to grow their skills to unprecedented levels, in
return for developing the next level of technologies. If
I joined them, they would use their influence to send
my family to the United States.

"Everything was concluded quickly, and I was
proud and eager to go in return for a safe and free
life for all of us. My parents assured me I'd join them
once I finished my two-year stint with The Organization and they'd established new identities. I soon
realized that would never come to pass."

Like all the boys The Organization took, he'd realized after the first hellish weeks that he was a slave
they had no intention of letting go, one they'd turn
into a mercenary and lethal weapon.

At first he'd refused to be of any use to them no

matter how much they tortured him, hoping they'd let him go. They'd only been too glad to escalate their abuse.

He exchanged a look with Antonio, filled with all the memories of their similar ordeals. "At one point I felt my mind and spirit breaking. I contemplated ending my life…and then you approached me."

Antonio had been a year younger, had introduced himself as Bones, as they'd been forbidden to use anything but the code names The Organization had given them. Antonio had already been selected for medicine because of his aptitudes—he'd been there since he was four. His friend had imparted on him the wisdom of his years with The Organization, convincing him to play along, so he'd become valued and be given privileges.

Then Antonio had offered him a lifeline. He'd asked him to join the brotherhood he belonged to. It was a group of boys selected and led by Numair, The Organization's top recruit, the older boy who'd been only known as Phantom then. Their secret brotherhood had become seven members when a year later their youngest member, Rafael, or Numbers, had joined them. The other three had been Raiden, or Lightning, Jakob, or Brainiac…and Cypher. None of them knew what he called himself now.

But when they'd been together, he'd taken their same vow: to become as skilled and knowledgeable as possible, so they'd one day escape, become powerful and wealthy enough to rule their own empires and bring down The Organization.

But meanwhile, they'd been The Organization's slaves and mercenaries, hired out to the highest bidder to execute any level of atrocities that no one else could: assassinations, sabotages, even starting revolutions, coups and wars.

It had taken over fifteen years to enact their escape plan. After they'd disappeared to build new personas, they'd surfaced to take the business world by storm and built Black Castle Enterprises, each presiding over his own segment of the global empire. Ivan ruled the cyber development world in ways that made his rivals call him Ivan the Terrible.

After they'd become established, and had begun untraceably dismantling The Organization, most of his Black Castle brothers had made finding their families or heritage a priority. Since most had come to The Organization too young to remember much, tracing their roots had been a lifelong endeavor. Ivan, though, knew his family and his brothers and had been certain that with his cyber reach, it would be the easiest thing in the world to find them once again.

But to his brothers' surprise he'd elected not to contact them. And he'd never told anyone, even Antonio, why.

He told him now. "I never told you this, but joining the brotherhood, and having your friendship, was what saved my sanity. Saved my life. You gave me a reason to live after my family's desertion made me want to give up."

A sharp breath expanded Antonio's chest. "You think…?"

"I *know*. The people I would have gladly laid my life down for, traded my life for theirs."

Antonio's eyes filled with the empathy of the profound connection they'd shared from that first day. "That's even worse than what my family did to me."

Antonio's aristocratic Italian family had thrown him away at birth, discarding their daughter's illegitimate child from a nobody. The Organization had taken him from the orphanage he'd ended up in. It seemed he considered abandoning a newborn to an unknown fate a lesser crime than giving up a grown son to a definitely hellish one.

Ivan exhaled. "Not that I can't excuse my parents. We could have all been killed, or worse, and I was their only bargaining chip. They were forced to make a choice between two evils. Sacrificing me was the lesser one. But knowing that rationally and accepting it emotionally was—is—worlds apart."

"Of course it is. If anyone should exact vengeance, it's you." Antonio sat forward, his frown ominous. "I want in on it."

Ivan waved away Antonio's aggression. "I don't want vengeance. Never did. All I wanted was to come to terms. I placed them under surveillance, learned everything about them since they abandoned me. The Organization followed through and set them up in the States with new identities. They've since changed those twice more. They've managed to completely hide from the Russian mafia, the former soviets and their benefactors at The Organization."

"But no one can hide from you," Antonio said, an edge of vicious satisfaction and pride in his voice.

That was indeed Ivan's specialty. He'd always hunted down the most elusive of quarries.

He nodded. "Since then their lives have been running smoothly and uneventfully. My three younger sisters and brother, who came to America very young, integrated totally. They have successful careers and stable personal lives. My parents, now John and Glenda Evans, have lives that are as respectable, comfortable and secure. It's as if I never existed to any of them. I live trying to forget them, too."

"You shouldn't." Antonio shredded the words through gritted teeth. "For parents to toss their firstborn to the sharks, to live a prosperous life at the price of his life... No, Ivan, this shouldn't go unpunished."

He shook his head. "But it will, Tonio. I don't have the thirst for retribution like you did."

Antonio's fists bunched as he visibly struggled to bring his outrage under control. "Let me know if you change your mind."

Ivan nodded, his throat tightening at his best friend's solidarity.

Antonio sat back, the gears of his formidable mind clearly changing. "But what does all this have to do with Anastasia and her brother?"

Ivan sipped his cooling coffee before putting his cup down, buying himself time to rein in the memories of his family and the devastation of their betrayal.

"They come in seven years ago," he finally said. "After five years out of The Organization's prison, with only you and our brothers as my sole human connections, I'd resigned myself I'd never have anyone outside of you. Then one day, during the first conference I sponsored, I met a blast from my past. A man I recognized at once as my pre-Organization childhood best friend.

"Alexei Mikhailov left Russia with his parents just days before I was sent to The Organization. It was one of the reasons I was so eager to leave. His parents, prominent scientists in soviet Russia, defected to the States and changed identities, too, becoming the Shepherds. The father, Sergei, became Michael, the mother Ludmila, Grace, and Alexei, who'd followed in his father's footsteps in the same branch of science in the States, became Alexander, or Alex. But because I'd changed too much…" They'd all made sure they did, so they'd be beyond recognition to their former captors even after they'd erased all evidence of their existence from their databases. "…Alex didn't recognize me. And I intended he never would. But I was still compelled to get closer. To my delight, even without knowing me, we hit it off all over again, resuming our former rapport as if the intervening years hadn't happened."

He paused, savoring the agony of the sweet memories. Then he went on. "Later that same night, I met Anastasia, Alex's younger sister, whom I remembered as a two-year-old child called Nastya, who used to be my youngest sister's playmate. She'd been twenty three years old then, and the most stunning creature I'd ever seen."

And the only woman he'd ever wanted, unstoppably, on sight.

From that first glance, the desire had been mutual and beyond either of them to resist...which they hadn't.

"For the next few weeks, as Alex and I became close friends again, I plunged into a passionate but secret affair with her." He leaned forward as echoes of this magical interlude that had never stopped haunting him deluged him again. Body hardening and heart thundering at the mere memories, he raked a hand through his hair, dragged himself back to the bleak reality. "I was overwhelmed by the ecstasy of being with her, not to mention by the delight of being with Alex again. Yet it haunted me that I might expose them to danger if one day the past caught up with me. And though that was my main fear, there was another problem.

"Through the escape and identity changes, not only had their family never lost contact with mine, they'd become like one family. My parents were like a second mother and father to them, with my sisters Anastasia's best friends and Alex in love with my youngest sister, Katerina, Cathy now. I knew being involved with Anastasia and Alex would bring my family crashing back into my life. My dread was validated when Alex kept trying to suck me into their extended family. It all came to a head when he asked me to be his best man."

He closed his eyes as memories of Alex, alive and

in love and eager for his closeness, tore at him all over again.

His breath left him on a ragged hiss. "I considered putting the past behind me, for his sake, for Anastasia's. But I couldn't do it. I was unable to bear the thought of being around my family again. It was the shove I needed to leave them alone. So I told Anastasia and Alex that I had inescapable business on his wedding day and withdrew from both their lives."

Silence lengthened in the wake of his last words.

Then Antonio asked, "Without explanation?"

He'd driven himself crazy ever since thinking how he could have handled it better. He'd always come to the same conclusion. "Any excuse I invented to explain my withdrawal would have only hurt more than letting them think I was just an unfeeling jerk."

Antonio inclined his head. "So now you don't want her going back to her life because you can't walk away again and you're worried your family might somehow recognize you when they eventually see you with her? Or are you afraid you'd change your mind about punishing them once you see them again?"

"Neither. The years haven't lessened my aversion to being anywhere near them, but intensified it. If she goes back to her family, I won't be able to be there for her anymore. And she still needs my support, my protection. She isn't ready to face the world without them yet." He leaned his elbows on his knees. "So now you have the reason you asked for."

After another beat of silence, Antonio rose to his feet. "I will still discharge her, Ivan."

Ivan heaved up to his feet, blood shooting to his head. "What? After what I just told you?"

"I actually now believe it's even more imperative to let her go back to her life."

"You bastard, you make me spill my guts—"

"Which you should have done ages ago. But what you told me only reinforces what I already decided." An outstretched arm aborted Ivan's outraged step forward. "When you first told me you'd be there for her during the hard journey back to her old self, I assumed she had no one else. But she has a family who loves her. She needs to go back to them, to bury her brother, so she'll get closure and start the healing process. Keeping her isolated with only you hovering over her is keeping her in a limbo of unresolved tension and grief."

"That's only your opinion."

"It's the truth. And there's also another reason why I will discharge her against your wishes."

"Brilliant. You have more bloody reasons to screw me over?"

"You always turn into Richard when you're frustrated." Before Ivan could blast him for likening him to that pain-in-the-ass Brit partner and former jailor of theirs, Richard Graves, Antonio sighed. "But yes, I do have another reason. You."

"Me?"

"Believe it or not, I'm stopping you from making a catastrophic mistake with the woman you care about." Antonio waited a moment to let his words settle on Ivan before he went on. "No matter how justified you think you are, the day she discovers you kept her away from her loved ones when she most needed them for your own ends, you'll find yourself in my same position with Liliana, with her feeling manipulated and betrayed, and with you unable to reach her again. And you already have a huge strike against you with her for the way you deserted her in the past. I don't want you to meet my same fate."

Ivan almost staggered back under the barrage of truths he hated to hear. "Dammit, Tonio. You were supposed to be too messed up to offer any resistance, let alone come up with a reasoned argument this ironclad."

"Just your luck I have a separate compartment in my head for my inner Vulcan." Antonio took him by the shoulders this time. "Let her go, Ivan. And after she's done what she needs to do, find a way to be there for her, to help her become strong and whole again, while staying out of your family's range."

Ivan's gaze held Antonio's grim one, aversion and dread bubbling up to the surface. "Do I even have a choice here?"

Antonio's attempted smile came out as a grimace. "None."

Anastasia was sitting by the window overlooking the ocean—the Pacific, since Ivan had mentioned they were somewhere in Los Angeles—when he and Dr. Balducci walked in.

Apart from a couple of nurses and orderlies she'd barely seen, those two had been her only company for the past five weeks. It sometimes felt as if she'd see no one else for the rest of her life except for the two men who'd saved her.

She watched them approaching her, and thought that if the gods came down from Mount Olympus, they wouldn't look that magnificent. She wondered again how they could look so much alike when one was one hundred percent Russian stock, like her, and the other was pure Italian. Their ethnicities were clear in their bone structure, but in their bodies, vibes and many other intangible things, they seemed to have been forged in the same higher-being manufacturing plant.

They stopped a couple of feet away, where the golden rays of a declining sun shining in through the window made them even more gorgeous. But though she mentally knew they were each other's equal, it was Ivan who embodied male beauty in her book. Or in her ledger. It felt as if everything that made her a female with these kinds of appreciations was frozen. Even gone.

Dr. Balducci spoke first. "Good news, Anastasia. I'm discharging you. I only ask that you resume your activities gradually and come to me when you can for a checkup. Of course, if you have any unusual symptoms, which I don't expect in the least, contact me at once. Ivan will provide you with every method to get hold of me day or night."

She blinked. "You mean…I—I can go?"

"Medically speaking, you're almost as good as new."

She hadn't even been considering her health. It wasn't what dictated whether she could go back.

Her gaze moved to the other juggernaut towering above her. Ivan's face was clamped in a disturbing expression.

"Is it okay for me to leave now?" She heard her voice wavering, imploring. "For my family to know… what happened?"

His eyes glittered a deeper green as a beat passed, and felt like an eternity, before he nodded. "Yes."

And the tears came again. As if they'd never stopped.

In her blurred gaze, she saw Dr. Balducci's image receding, and Ivan's hovering a breath away. But he didn't offer any comfort, just stood there, fists at his sides.

All she wanted was to throw herself at him, seek the shelter of his infinite strength, his encompassing protection. But she held back. She couldn't need him or lean on him any more than she already had. Ivan, from devastating experience, didn't stick around, and this time when he eventually left, it wouldn't be like before.

Seven years ago she'd been young and resilient. She'd suffered an indelible scar when he'd walked away, but she'd survived, even thrived. This time, in her bereft and damaged state, if her dependence deepened even more, she feared she'd be unable to recover.

Finally, feeling too wrecked to shed another tear, she slumped back in her seat limply, looking up at him. His gaze flayed her with its intensity. Yet he still said nothing.

She finally pushed to her feet. "Can I have my things back now, please?" she asked him. "I need them so I can arrange my return to New York. As for—for..."

He took an urgent step forward as she choked, and for a second, she thought he'd take her in his arms. He didn't.

Looking as if the words were being torn out of him, he said, "Don't worry about anything. I will deliver you—and Alex—to your family."

Three

"What will we tell my family?"

Ivan looked up from his laptop at her subdued question. Anastasia had been trying to get herself to ask it ever since they'd left Dr. Balducci's secret medical installation and driven to a private airstrip to board Ivan's jet.

Until now, all she'd managed had been monosyllabic answers to his constant questions whether she needed anything.

Not that she possibly could. As he'd been doing for the past five weeks, he'd kept anticipating her needs, and far beyond. He'd barely let her feet touch the ground all the way to this luxurious seat in his state-of-the-art jet, barely let her lift a hand. The most she'd gotten away with had been going to the bathroom under her own power and feeding herself.

To escape his persistent focus and care, she'd had to pretend to fall asleep. Even then, she'd felt his gaze on her, no doubt counting her breaths, as usual.

She'd ended up falling asleep for real, and had just awoken a minute ago to find him finally doing something other than watch her. She'd been tempted to leave him engrossed in whatever he was doing. But she'd had to ask that question. They had to be on the same page during the coming ordeal.

It hadn't even occurred to her that he'd offer to take her home. But she'd still felt his aversion to the task and tried to convince him to let her go back alone. It had only made him more adamant that she was in no condition to deal with the upheaval ahead. Not to mention that only he could navigate the sensitive time until Alex was buried.

Now caught once more in his burning focus, she wished she'd kept silent. He closed the laptop, pushed aside the adjustable table and sat forward in the seat facing hers.

"Now that those responsible for Alex's murder have paid—"

She had to interrupt, her sluggish heart starting to hammer. "How exactly did they pay?"

His gaze stilled on her face. "You're sure you want details?"

She hadn't before. But now she burned for them. "Yes."

He didn't answer at once, as if trying to gauge if it

was prudent to give her more information that might disturb her.

But he must have seen the steel hardening her nerves, the fire licking through her veins, her need to have vengeance for Alex fueling her, overriding any aversion she might have previously had to learn what he was capable off, what he'd done.

He finally gave a nod of acknowledgment. "Your immediate boss at FuturEn and insiders within the International Energy Organization had been exposed. Not for the crime Alex discovered—that they'd made sure his results would be publicly falsified, discredited and never see application, while bribing all energy competitors with the threat that those results were indeed a breakthrough that could deprive them of a big percentage of the market within years. And not for what they'd done to him—and you—since that will always remain a secret for your protection. I exposed every other crime they'd ever committed, which were many and equally as heinous. They'll never know who exposed them, but the evidence I made available to the authorities is copious and conclusive. They've been arrested and the dates of their expedited trials set. They've lost everything and won't see the outside of a maximum-security prison in this life."

"That's all?"

A chilling smile touched his lips as if he recognized and approved of her lust for a harsher punishment. "No. Those who gave the order to end your and Alex's lives will be locked up with their worst nightmares—those who owe them pain and suffering, and others who'll contribute imaginative punishments for one price or another. Those men will either meet their demise after protracted abuse or, worse, be deprived of its mercy."

She closed her eyes, struggling to suppress the vicious satisfaction that charred her blood. She was ferociously glad those monsters would pay, and that their punishment would be long and agonizing, and preferably unending.

It amazed her all over again that she was capable of such ruthlessness, that she would have exacted that punishment herself if she could have. She knew if Ivan hadn't taken action, she would have done anything to avenge Alex's death. But relying on the law wouldn't have done her any good. As a weak adversary with flimsy evidence, she would have gotten nowhere and ultimately would have been forced to resort to reckless measures. Which would have proven as ineffective and probably ended up in disaster for her and for her family, too.

So Ivan had saved her yet again, this time from the consequences of the vengeance she would have done anything to get, but wasn't equipped to enact. He'd given it to her, full and final, without a price for her or her loved ones.

Gratitude flooded her, along with so many other emotions that she felt she'd burst with it all. Needing an outlet, she reached a shaky hand to cover both of his as they interlaced loosely between his knees.

It was the first time she'd touched him in over

seven years. And though it was nothing like that first touch that had changed her forever, that had told her this was the only man she'd ever crave, it was still as potent in its own way. The powerful hands that were capable of so much passion, skill and damage seemed to buzz beneath her trembling touch. His gaze crowded with so much she couldn't fathom.

She let out all her emotions on a quivering breath. "Thank you."

The stiffening of his body and face was an admonition, reminding her he'd demanded she never thank him.

"But I need to far more than thank you," she persisted. "For this. For everything you've done. And now for taking me—taking us—home." She shied away from thinking of Alex's body in the belly of the plane so she could go on. "Especially when I feel how much you'd rather not."

Sitting back, he moved his hands out of reach, a startled look coming into his eyes. No doubt he was surprised that she picked up on his reluctance.

He only said, "Alex was my friend, Anastasia."

The barely checked emotions that radiated from him whenever Alex was mentioned hit her full force again. Was that the reason for his reluctance? He hated that they were taking Alex home in a casket, to bury him? Did he feel, like her, that goodbye would feel real only then? Did it hurt him, too?

If it hurt him a fraction of how it hurt her, then it made sense. And it again rewrote everything she'd thought she'd known for the past seven years.

Ivan's friendship with Alex had lasted as long as their own relationship had. Exactly ten weeks. At the time, she'd believed the two men had shared a deep connection. Then his desertion had forced her to revise her opinion.

Though their liaisons had been brief, Ivan had left a gaping void in both their lives. Each had mourned his loss, had struggled with their own interpretation of its causes.

Alex had been resigned that someone of Ivan's caliber would surely not find him worthy of more than a passing acquaintance, that he'd been delusional to think they'd built the foundation of a lifelong friendship. As for herself, she thought she'd been nothing but another notch on his bedpost. Why else would he have simply walked away?

But after everything that had happened in the last weeks, after realizing he'd kept such close tabs on them, she was forced to reconsider everything. It was clear there was far more to this whole thing than she'd thought. Far, far more to Ivan. What, she couldn't even guess at. And if he never told her, she'd never know.

But for now, she had to tell him what Alex hadn't had the chance to.

"He was your friend, too, Ivan. He never got over your sudden disappearance from his life, yet always treasured the time he had with you."

It was agony to talk about Alex in the past tense, as she would from now on. And equally painful to reveal an intensely personal secret of his that only she'd known.

But Ivan had to know it. It was about him, and after all he'd done, she couldn't withhold it from him.

The next moment she wished she had. That look in his eyes as he met hers was filled with unbearable pain. The same look she'd seen before he'd declared he would deliver her and Alex to their family.

What did it all mean? How did his behavior, past and present, add up? Because it simply didn't.

Or maybe it did. Maybe he felt bad about the way he'd exited their lives, the remorse compounded by what had happened to them, by what he'd been unable to stop. Maybe he was appeasing his guilt by trying to put right as much as he could of this mess.

Not that it mattered what he felt or why he was doing this. For reasons he kept to himself, Ivan was hell-bent on seeing this tragedy to its resolution.

And though having him so near was like a dull scalpel opening old scars and new wounds, she was more grateful than she could ever express. She couldn't have survived without him. And once they broke the tragic news to their family, only his presence would get her through their grief.

After an oppressive silence, Ivan made no comment on her revelation and answered her original question. "I advise against taking anyone into your confidence about what happened, no matter how tempted you are. Not now, not ever. I've erased all evidence of the crime so I could deal with its perpetrators without repercussions. Any knowledge of it outside of us can someday cause untold trouble. I've constructed an airtight scenario to be told to the world, starting with your families, and I need you to always be consistent in telling it."

She nodded, hit again by how sinister this all was, how much larger than anything she'd ever thought she'd encounter in her life.

His eyes filled with approval of her unquestioning acceptance. Then he went on. "You'll say neither you nor Alex knew which arm of the government recruited you for the top secret project, that all had gone smoothly, that you were supposed to go home when you were involved in a helicopter crash two weeks ago. The pilot died at once, Alex was gravely injured, while you had the least injuries."

She gave another nod as she absorbed the details that mixed reality with fiction. "How will I explain your role in all this?"

"You'll say I'm a previous acquaintance you contacted because I'm Dr. Balducci's partner, who transported you to his facility. But it was those in charge of your mission who didn't clear you to contact your family before now. You'll tell the truth, that Antonio operated on both of you, but could only save you, downplaying your injuries so you could be in this condition after two weeks. Part of the misdirection to the culprits is creating a different time line."

Her head spun at his scenario, what she'd now have to act out for the rest of her life. Not even their parents or Cathy would ever know the truth about how or why Alex died.

He went on. "That all said, I want you to say as little as possible from now on. To start, let me do the explaining."

Another surge of gratitude swept through her. "I'd prefer that, too. I doubt anyone will question anything you'll say."

"If anyone does, or if any authority investigates, I made sure all threads would lead to various government arms that no one would question. I made sure that each agency would have no way of making sure which one you were working for and would assume you were working for one of the others."

She shook her head in amazement. "How? How did you do all that?"

"I *am* in the business of monitoring, controlling and even creating records and information. No one will ever know the truth, and you'll be forever safe from any fallout." She swallowed, flabbergasted yet again at another demonstration of his power. He sat forward, enveloping her in the heat of his body and aura. "Apart from all that, I assure you of another thing. Alex will be honored, his research and results will all be published. His legacy, which is substantial, will be applied, will get the recognition and rewards it deserves. His family will be given their full benefit, morally and financially."

The urge to launch herself at him, bury her face into his endless chest, cling and sob her heart out, almost overpowered her. Her every frailty reached out to absorb all she could of his strength. What he was so unreservedly offering.

Only her depletion and mounting dread of the impending reunion stopped her, made her unable to seek his refuge.

Which was just as well, since his offer of solace and protection didn't seem to extend to anything physical.

And she had to abide by his rules—this man she'd once loved, who'd injured her in the past and healed her in the present, both with no explanation.

But she didn't need to understand him to give him his due. It was what Alex would have wanted her to do. "Alex couldn't have hoped to leave his legacy in the hands of anyone better or more capable than you."

His eyes darkened again, whether at the mention of Alex's name or at the implied gratitude in her statement.

Before he could respond, she asked, "How long before we land?"

His turbulent gaze flitted to his phone. "Two hours."

She lowered her seat back to a flat position, pulled the blanket over her aching body. "I'll sleep again, then."

He surged forward, helping her adjust the seat and the covers. "Do that. Rest."

You'll need it went unspoken.

Ivan watched Anastasia sleeping, and knowing this would be the last time he did had bleakness expanding in his chest.

They'd landed an hour ago, but he couldn't bring

himself to interrupt her sleep. As restless as it was, it was still better than what she'd go through when she woke up. This way, he had her beneath his eyes, where he could ward off the world, for as long as possible.

That had been one of the reasons he was escorting her home—to prolong his time with her. As Antonio had said, that was for himself as much as it was for her.

But the main reason he was doing this remained her, and Alex. Antonio had been right. He couldn't keep her any longer from the people she loved, those who were her lifelong support system. She needed her family, needed to bury her brother, give them all the chance to grieve, to say goodbye.

And he couldn't stomach letting her take the brunt of her family's shock alone. He couldn't bear that Alex would be buried without him being there. His abhorrence to being close to his family had been outweighed by his need to shield her, to honor Alex.

Now he had to rouse her. And they both had to plunge into their own version of a waking nightmare.

Two hours later, Ivan stood behind Anastasia on the threshold of the home Alex had shared with his wife, Ivan's sister, and their two children, his niece and nephew.

As they waited for the door to open, he felt Anastasia swaying, as if she was coming apart under the weight of the dread of confronting her best friend. And though it hurt to touch her, his hand clamped her trembling arm, offering her his strength, letting her know he'd step in anytime she needed.

In the next moment, he wondered if it was he who needed support.

The woman who opened the door had an eager smile that, in spite of all the changes twenty-eight years had wrought, was still the same as that of the baby sister he'd known. Her smile immediately froze when she saw Anastasia without Alex, looking desolate, and with him, a stranger, towering over her.

To say the next hour was harrowing would be to say that his time with The Organization hadn't been too bad.

At first, Anastasia had haltingly introduced him, so she wouldn't break down on the spot, needing to be strong for her best friend and sister-in-law. Then Katerina's—Cathy's—questions had come, the dread mounting until each answer fleshed out the scenario he'd created, validating her worst possible fears.

Then the agony had come. He'd felt every stab of it in his own gut as he watched yet another person he cared about in the throes of absolute anguish. For just seeing his sister in the flesh had brought back the memories of how much he'd loved her, from the moment his mother had told him she was pregnant again. In spite of her maturation from his Russian baby sister into a thoroughly American woman, she was still somehow his little Katerina.

He'd thought nothing could be worse than being ambushed by those kindred feelings he hadn't thought he could ever feel again, or than suffering shearing empathy for her loss. Until her—and his—parents arrived.

Seeing the man and woman he'd once loved completely, whom he'd idolized, rush to their bereaved daughter's side, seemingly as overcome, rocked him to his core.

For almost three decades, since he'd discovered what they'd done to him, he'd imagined how he'd feel if he ever saw them again. He'd come up with a thousand scenarios. He'd known he'd hate it, had been determined never to expose himself to it. But he'd thought he'd braced for each possibility, that none could actually hit him too hard.

He'd been wrong.

After their desperate attempts to contain their daughter's agony, their focus had converged on him. He'd thought he was being too sensitive to their merest glance, but none of those who'd flooded the house, including his other sisters and brother, had looked at him like that.

As if they recognized him.

But of course they couldn't. Nothing remained of the twelve-year-old they'd bartered away for their freedom but his eye color. And then how would they even suspect a resemblance, when they must have believed him long dead?

A big percentage of the boys culled by The Organization couldn't endure their brutal training. Of those who did, more than half didn't last in the field. It was why they were always harvesting more, with their mortality rate so high. And the boy his parents knew, the slight nerd he'd been, wouldn't have been able to survive the inferno he'd been tossed in. If it hadn't been for his brothers, he wouldn't have.

He'd waited for anger to overtake him, but all he felt was desolation. Even now, he couldn't hate them. The only thing he felt when he looked at them—older, frailer and in their grief, even fragile—was pity.

There was no doubt in his mind they'd loved Alex as a son. Instead of that making him more bitter, it was like a knife of sympathy tearing through his guts.

The ordeal continued into the next day. Everyone, as if responding to his superior powers, let him steer everything. He'd fast-forwarded the process and arranged for the burial, laying Alex's body to rest, along with the true circumstances of his death.

Now they were back at Alex's house, and the true grieving had just begun. Alex's parents and Katerina seemed to be sinking deeper into despair. The only one who'd already gone through the stages of loss was Anastasia, and he felt her pour out her support to everyone who needed her. As he'd feared she would. But there was nothing he could do to stop that, to make her preserve herself, not give too much.

He now stood at the periphery of the jarringly sunny living room watching those who'd loved Alex flocking around his family in an effort to absorb a measure of their distress.

Then the agitation that had been rising and falling in jagged waves since they'd arrived crested again. The three people whose very presence tossed him from one level of turmoil to a higher one were approaching him.

Anastasia, and his parents.

The one who addressed him, puffy-eyed and broken, was his mother. "Mr. Konstantinov, Ana told us everything you've done for her and Alex. We—we wanted to thank you, even if there's nothing we could possibly say to express our gratitude."

"But we *are* grateful, beyond expression, on behalf of everyone." That was his father, looking nothing like the imposing figure he remembered, smaller, weaker, even helpless in his anguish. "Thank you, son."

He'd once had a bomb shower him with shrapnel, almost tearing his leg right off. The word *son* from the father who'd given him away tore through him with far more force and pain.

His reaction must have shown, for Anastasia came between them, no doubt mistaking it for his dislike of thank-yous. "Ivan has a big problem with accepting thanks, so if you really want to express your gratitude, don't."

"But of course we have to express it," his mother exclaimed, her eyes, glittering with tears as they fixed on his face, with something that was feverish in its intensity in their depths. A…question? "And if there's ever anything at all we can do for you, we'd only be too happy and grateful to do it, my dear."

The sheer kindness and eagerness in her expression, what was reflected in his father's face as they awaited his response, felt like more stabs to his heart.

He could barely hold back from shouting, *All I*

ever wanted was for you not to abandon me to a life of servitude.

As if feeling his critical condition, Anastasia intervened again. "I bet there's nothing we mere mortals can ever do for Ivan." His parents insisted that even the most powerful people had to need something, but she cut across their protests. "I'm sure if this is true, he won't hesitate to ask. You can count on him to make his wishes known, right, Ivan?"

He found himself nodding, his gaze riveted on her face, mesmerized by what he saw. A glimpse of his old Anastasia, the woman who'd glowed with life and candor, who'd captured him from the first glance.

"But as you know," she continued, "Ivan has already gone above and beyond and now he needs to go back to the life he's put on hold for so long to be there for us."

Clearly torn between disappointment that he'd leave and not wanting to impose on him, both his parents deluged him again with thanks and persistent hopes that he'd return whenever possible. It was all he could do to answer them coherently, then walk, not run, away from them.

His whole being in chaos, he felt Anastasia fall into step with him as he headed to the door. From her wary sidelong glances, it was clear she felt something was not right here, but was at a loss as to what it was and what had provoked it.

Not that he was about to explain. All he wanted now was to bolt as far away as possible from this place. Preferably to the ends of the earth, where he'd never lay eyes on his parents or the rest of his family ever again.

It would also serve Anastasia's purpose, too. It hadn't only been to save him from an uncomfortable situation that Anastasia had suggested he go. Clearly she, too, wanted him to leave. After all the time she'd been limited to only his company, she must have had way more than enough of it. Not to mention that he remained the odd man out here, and in this, of all times, she must be eager to be alone with her family.

But how could he just walk away this time, when he never wanted to leave her side again?

There was more to this than being unable to bear the thought of not seeing her again. Though she was out of danger, it was still a long road to complete recovery, physically and, more importantly, emotionally. She was outwardly holding together, being there for her parents, for Katerina, for the rest of the family, but he knew she was crumbling inside. And it wasn't only the brutal loss of Alex, but her own ordeal. Most probably she'd suffer one degree or another of post-traumatic stress.

But he couldn't help her himself now. If he stayed around to do so, he'd be too disturbed being in the vicinity of his family to offer her the stability she now needed. The best thing he could do was to make sure she had the best specialists to help her deal with the psychological repercussions. But he could not stay.

As she led him outside, he caught her arm in a gentle grip, stopping her.

The eyes that turned up to his were reddened, the

lids swollen, her gaze hesitant and fragile. Yet those eyes were the most beautiful sight he'd ever seen, the most powerful weapon. They tore through his being with more force than bullets had torn through his flesh. For they made him want everything he couldn't have. They made him weak. They overpowered him when nothing else ever had.

Fighting the overpowering compulsion to crush her to him, feeling as if shards of glass filled his throat, he said, "I know you have your family now, and that you never ask for help, but…I am here for you. Don't let your independence or any other consideration stop you from letting me know what you need, now or at any time in the future. Promise me that if you need anything, anything at all, you'll ask me for it."

Her gaze clung to his, brightening with tears again, her still pale lips quivering in a semblance of a smile. "If I think it's something you can do, sure."

"I can and will do anything."

Her eyes darkened and a faint flush spread over her now sharper cheekbones, seeping into her dainty lips as they opened on a tiny, sharp inhalation. He had no idea how he stopped himself from snatching her into his arms and devouring her.

Then with a nod that encompassed reluctance and acquiescence at once, she accepted his carte blanche.

Though he doubted she'd ever use it. He'd just have to keep watching her, even closer this time, and do a far better job at anticipating her needs and protecting her from the dangers of the world.

Then it was the moment. His role had ended, and

his one-time pass back into her life had expired. He had to let go. Until she needed him again. Knowing her, barring another catastrophe, that would be never.

Knowing her loss would be a worse injury than what he'd suffered in the past, knowing he'd never recover from it, he said what he hadn't the first time he'd walked away.

"Goodbye, Anastasia."

Four

But I can't say goodbye. Not again.

The words kept reverberating in Anastasia's mind. Long after Ivan had brushed past her and walked to the limo that awaited him in the driveway. Long after it disappeared down the street.

And though the protest had exploded in her head when he'd said goodbye, out loud she'd said nothing. As if not saying goodbye herself wouldn't make his real.

Instead, she'd just watched him go, willing him to turn, to say something else that wouldn't make this final. Some promise he'd be back later, to at least check up on her. That this time he wouldn't disappear from her life completely. That he'd leave the door ajar.

Leaving it up to her to approach him, and only with a need, slammed it shut, this time forever.

Because she'd never ask anything of him.

But he hadn't turned, not to qualify his goodbye, not even to give her one last look. She'd watched his limo until it turned the corner, still feverishly hoping that the man who hadn't let her out of his sight for five weeks wouldn't go like that. She had no idea how long she'd stood there before her hammering heart had slowed to the rhythm of resignation, the knowledge of the centerpiece fact she'd now have to build her new shattered life around.

He was never coming back.

It felt like her world had ended, for a third time. Two out of the three times it had happened, it had been on Ivan's account.

But it wasn't her world that mattered now. Her family needed her. It was what had finally made her walk back into the house full of all who'd loved Alex, where she'd plunged again in the surreal realm of being in his house knowing he'd never be there again. Being among the people she'd been closest to since birth, contemplating all the ways their lives would be diminished and distorted in his absence had agonized her more with each passing second. But it had at least made it impossible to think of Ivan.

After a while, the presence of the mourners had turned from solace to suffocation for her parents and Cathy. As the one who'd dealt with the most brutal stages of Alex's loss, it was up to her to take charge. Using up her last traces of stamina and diplomacy, she'd made everyone leave, put the shattered Cathy and kids to bed and taken her broken parents home.

Once she'd settled them down as best she could, and sought the sanctuary of her own room, she'd finally taken off the mask of strength. Closing the door behind her, she'd collapsed where she'd stood, letting misery drown her again.

Gone. Alex was *gone*.

And Ivan, too.

She'd lost him all over again.

Not that she'd ever had him. He'd only reentered her life on a mission. Once it was accomplished, there was no more reason for him to stick around. Now she knew why this demolished her.

When he'd been by her side day and night, she hadn't been able to think ahead to the point in time when he'd leave again. She'd gotten so used to him being there it had felt as if the day would never come. That was why it had been such a shock when he'd not only walked away, but had also seemed as if he couldn't bear being around her anymore, couldn't wait to leave her behind.

That was what hurt until she couldn't breathe. What made her feel as if the ground had been swept out from under her, making her feel she was plummeting into an abyss. Not only had he removed his support, but also his fervor to be around her.

But no matter how vulnerable and lost she felt without him, she knew it would have been worse if he hadn't ended it now. Any longer with him, any more dependence on him, and his ultimate departure might have killed her. At least this way, she had a chance of survival.

Not that survival seemed like such a good thing now. For the few days since he'd left, she'd been going through the motions of living. Staying in both Alex's home and her parents', helping them with everyday chores, pretending things like food and homework and bath time and laundry mattered. Trying to ameliorate the unbearable. For herself and for them.

And it wasn't working. She only felt worse as every minute dragged by, Alex's absence solidifying into a gaping crater in her heart, a closed fist in her right side and a missing vital ingredient in her every breath.

Alex hadn't just been her older brother, he'd been her best friend, mentor, partner and confidant. Every single thing in her life was inextricably entwined with him. He'd been more to her than he'd been to their parents, to his wife and children. All of them had parts of them, interests and activities, that hadn't included him. She hadn't. He'd even been her squash and gym partner. And she didn't know how to plug the holes now that he'd been ripped from her. The feeling of being torn in half constantly gushed in, leaving her sinking.

But it was only in the last couple of days that others began noticing her condition. Though their anguish kept deepening, Cathy and her parents were slowly recovering their ability to think, at least enough to see beyond their own turmoil.

Though they didn't know the depth of her injuries—

and never would—they now thought she was the one who had the most healing to do, and they said they would see to it. Just now they'd insisted she go home and rest. Making them promise to call her if anyone needed anything, she'd finally succumbed.

On her way home, she pulled into a shopping mall parking lot. She had no idea how long she sat staring ahead, trying to empty her mind, to not focus on Alex or her endless memories with him since the day she'd been born.

But not thinking about Alex only let her mind think of the other man who dominated her every waking and sleeping moment. Ivan.

It was like watching a movie of her life's transformative moments. For he'd been there in each and every one of them. Their cause or their conclusion.

Every moment replayed in her mind and impacted her senses. When he'd first walked up to her, looking like a supreme being right out of a fantasy. When he'd pulled her into that first kiss, an overwhelming seduction. When he'd loomed above her, invading her body with pleasure, branding her as his, a storm of passion in human form. When he'd snatched her from death's cold pull, like a lethal archangel. When he'd given her the only reason powerful enough to cling to life, imbuing her with his endless strength, like a guardian angel.

The images played in a loop, but always snagged on a specific one. His face filling with colliding emotions as he'd said goodbye. Watching it over and over as she sat there, she took it apart, looked at it from every angle, until she finally realized something.

How hard it had been for him to say it.

Jerking out of her stupor, she fumbled out her phone, her heart starting to thunder as she searched out the direct number he'd saved on it. She hit Dial as she restarted the car. He answered after only one ring.

"Anastasia?"

To everyone she was Ana. Only he called her by her full name. Every time he said it, he filled the simple utterance with so much, it filled volumes in her being. She'd once thought she'd heard how much he wanted her, and everything else he'd felt in the way he said it. She'd since come to believe she'd been only hearing what she'd wanted to hear.

But there was no mistaking how he'd said her name now. It was the very sound of agitation and solicitude combined. He was worried she needed something, and that it was big enough only he could deal with it, important enough to make her call him.

Before she could reassure him, his urgency silenced her. "I just hit Dial and the phone rang instead."

Did she get that right? "You were calling me?"

"I went to Alex's house and your mother told me you went home, but I arrived here and didn't find you. I was calling you when your call connected first. What happened? Where are you?"

He'd been looking for her? Was at her home now? Why?

"Anastasia."

His bark was pure anxiety now, clearly imagining another disaster had befallen her.

She rushed to allay his concern. "Nothing happened. I—I just stopped somewhere on the way." He didn't need to know that she had only sit there staring at a memory reel starring him. But *she* needed to know one thing. "Why were you looking for me?"

There was a long beat of silence on the other end, before his deep voice poured into her brain again, and his words snuffed out any light that remained in her world.

"I wanted to see you again before I went back to Russia."

Anastasia didn't even remember the drive back home.

Her brain registered nothing until she saw him sitting in his car outside her family home, like a predator lying in wait. He got out as soon as she neared, looking like a god descended to earth with the setting sun behind him. Even from a distance she felt the tension radiating from him. It swamped her as she drove past him into the garage, as he opened her door and helped her out.

Her throat tightening, her heart hammering, she invited him into the house. Every nerve fired with his nearness, with the intensity blasting from him.

Needing air, she led him all the way out back to her favorite part of her mother's garden—the gazebo. It was where she'd sat alone countless times with her laptop or a book, where her mind had always ended up dwelling on the man she'd loved and lost. She turned to him now.

He towered over her, his eyes that hypnotic green she'd always drowned in, his expression singeing her blood with its heat. And she just couldn't do it.

She couldn't let him say goodbye. Not yet.

Not before she said what she'd called him to say.

"Anastasia—"

"I could have died, Ivan." Her quavering words cut off what he'd begun to say. "But I didn't. Because you saved me. Now I need one more thing from you."

He took a step closer, tight, barely leashed power in the move. Power she felt could move mountains, as he'd done for her and Alex. "Anything, Anastasia. Tell me what you need."

"I need you to show me that I didn't just survive, Ivan. I need you to prove to me that I'm still alive."

His eyes flared with such a blaze of emotions, she almost needed to shield her eyes. "Anastasia…"

This time he said her name as if it hurt, the inflection filled with seething hesitation. And she knew he wouldn't make a move. Either because he couldn't credit what she'd asked him for, or because he was taking it upon himself to protect her from any recklessness in her weakened, needy state.

But she couldn't take no for an answer. This was the one thing she needed. The last thing she'd have of him.

He'd nurtured her back to physical health, but she now needed a salve for her emotions, a reviving dose of passion from the only man she'd ever been intimate with.

Her move ate up the distance between them as a trembling hand rose to his face. The moment she cupped his rugged jaw and felt his strength fill her palm, overflow into her being it was like the years apart evaporated. Nothing remained inside her but longing, and it had taken only this contact to break the dam and have it all come pouring out.

"I need this, Ivan," she whispered. "I need you."

His flesh buzzed beneath her hand, electrifying her. "How could you? I left you—"

"It doesn't matter what you did or why you did it. The past is gone. Alex is gone." She stifled a sob that threatened to tear through her. "But I'm still here. And it's terrible, Ivan. Terrible to be alone, to know I'll always be alone because I'll never be able to share what happened, what changed me forever, with another person for the rest of my life."

"*Bozhe moi*, Anastasia."

He'd only ever spoken Russian when he'd lost his hold on his rigid control in the throes of passion and pleasure. But now different emotions compromised his control, eliciting his tormented "My God."

Her hand trembled around his neck, her fingers plunging into his luxurious mane. "But I share it with you, Ivan. It's only because you know everything, that you've lived it with me that I'm able to go on. And I want to share more with you, what might bring me back to life. The past is gone—"

"The past may be gone, but there's tomorrow—"

A finger on his lips stopped his protest, her tear-soaked voice breaking. "There's only now. And you said you'd do anything. That's the only thing I need. The one thing I'll ever ask of you."

His chest expanded, as if bracing under an insupportable burden. Not only wasn't he unfeeling, as she'd once thought, she now realized he probably felt too much, had to close himself off, to protect himself, and maybe the whole world from the power of his emotions. She'd seen him when a measure of these emotions—the violent, vengeful ones—had been let loose. He'd been lethal. She no longer doubted that he'd wreaked far more destruction in his life, that what she'd witnessed had only been the tip of the iceberg. And now she was chipping away at the barrier that restrained his devastating potential, and it was about to crack.

Not that it worried her. She wanted him to demolish her with all the ferocity of his fervor. He'd only ever hurt her when he'd deprived her of it.

"You need this, too, Ivan. You lost him, too." His flinch was proof that Alex's loss did hurt him. Her hand twisted in his hair in answering agony. "I need to share his loss with you, the one who knows, the one strong enough to live with it. And I'm the only one you can share it with, the one who understands, who's been part of it all."

The torment that blazed on his face solidified her belief.

He mourned Alex, almost as deeply as she did.

"Anastasia, you don't know what it takes for me

to be like this." Like this? In control? Holding back? "You don't know what you're risking."

"I have nothing more to risk, Ivan."

His head tilted back against her hand, a growl rumbling deep in his chest, as if there was a trapped, starving beast there. He *was* resisting because he feared he'd hurt her.

She had to make him believe he wouldn't, had to make him stop holding back. Her other hand slipped around his neck, coaxing his face down to hers. "The only injury I could have sustained was letting you go without being with you one more time."

She lowered her arms to hug all she could of him, a breath she'd been holding for seven long years flowing out of her in tortured relief. Until he stiffened in her embrace as if she'd electrocuted him.

Oh, God. This could mean she'd gotten it all wrong. That he didn't need comfort, at least not from her. That when he'd said he'd give her anything she needed, he hadn't thought it would be him—the one thing he hadn't offered.

Before she could withdraw in mortification, his formidable body surrendered to her hold. He still didn't embrace her, but he gave her license to hug him. So she did. Hug him and hug him. His sighs were the very sound of agonized enjoyment. They reverberated deep in her marrow as he rested his forehead on hers, swaying with her to the erratic cadence of their heartbeats.

Then suddenly he was pushing away. Before let-down burned her to ashes, she was swept up in his arms. Where she'd despaired of ever being again.

Forgetting to breathe as he strode inside the house, she savored the weightlessness, the powerlessness, the soaring he always made her feel when he carried her like this.

His effortless steps paused halfway up the stairs to the upper floor and he looked down at her, his eyes probing hers. "This is what you want?"

Instead of answering him, she nestled her head more securely against his chest. "My bedroom is the last door in the corridor."

That rumble of voracity that had always melted her revved beneath her ear. He hurried through the upper floor that was all her living space, crossing inside her bedroom in seconds. The moment he closed the door, he let her slide down on his hard body and pressed her against it, letting her feel how the tremors shaking her body echoed in his.

Unable to wait another heartbeat, her hands convulsed in his hair, her lips gasping for his. The moment she reached them, she took them in a wrenching kiss, every moist glide and thrust of her tongue confessing how much she'd longed for him. It reminded her how much she'd lost, how much she'd lose again.

But she had him now, and she would hoard all she could of him.

She'd barely started when he tore his lips away. Crying out, she surged up, desperate for his breath so she could breathe, for his heartbeat so her heart wouldn't stop, needing his taste to fill her up for the desolate future without him.

But he'd only broken the kiss to melt more down her neck, her breasts. His growls of pleasure and need were elemental, set off jolts of hunger in her core.

He wanted her now. She knew he did. With all his indomitable, magnificent being. For now. And she wanted to have every spark of his desire, needed it. Had to have it. If even for one hour.

Too weak still to climb him and wrap herself around him, she could only stand on tiptoe and arch back, offering all of her. Her legs buckled when his erection pressed into her core through their clothes. Moaning, she ground against him, pressing his head harder into her aching breasts. He opened his mouth over her sweatshirt-smothered flesh, nipping one of her nipples.

A cry tore from her as she bucked with pleasure, losing all coherence. "Ivan, please, just *take* me."

With another growl, he picked her up again and carried her where she'd never thought she'd have him—her bed.

His gaze raked every inch of her, igniting her skin wherever it lingered, then he came down over her, his arms a prison of muscle around her. She breathed in the scent of his maleness and protectiveness, fiery and clean and musky. Her mouth watered then her stomach rumbled.

"You're hungry." He pulled back, gaze sharp, tone accusing. He'd constantly worried she didn't have enough food, kept urging her to eat more.

He started to get up and she clutched his hand, the hand that had snatched her from death's jaws, that had taught her what pleasure really was. "Not for food, Ivan."

"Anastasia…" he groaned as he sank back into her arms.

She singed her lips with his heat as she ran them over his cheekbones, his jaw, his neck, loving the feel of the few days' worth of beard he now wore.

At its soft abrasion, she moaned into his skin. "All I want is to feast on you."

And she did, trembling with the enormity of having him in her arms again. Her hands roamed the breadth of his back, reveled in the leashed power of his arms, her lips and tongue delighted in skimming every inch she could reach, every touch and taste everything she'd craved for years. *Years*.

But he broke away from her again, to blaze a possessive trail down her body. He had her writhing in pleasure as he seemed to melt her clothes off. It was only when she found herself naked beneath him in what felt like seconds that self-consciousness assaulted her.

Dr. Balducci had done a masterful job on the scar that traversed her abdomen. It reminded her she'd been taken apart and put back together inside, but she'd gotten used to seeing it, mostly dismissed it. But having Ivan's hands and eyes on it, she felt as if it was the ugliest thing ever, and that it covered her from head to toe.

On a mental level, she knew Ivan would sympathize. But on the sensual one, the male in him, what she knew from ecstatic experience was ferociously carnal and exacting, had to be put off by it.

But as she tried to reach for her comforter to cover herself, Ivan, still fully clothed, captured her wrists. He pinned them beside her head, his knees imprisoning her thighs.

"Don't hide from me, *moya dusha*."

At hearing him call her *my soul*, one of the extravagant endearments he'd used to lavish on her, she sobbed, "I don't want you to see me like this."

Letting go of one of her wrists, his hand went to her chin, making her meet his gaze. "This scar?" His other hand shook as it traced it. "It pains me to see it, as a reminder I could have lost you. But it's also precious because it's proof you survived. And it's beautiful, like every other part of you."

Unable to bear him taking pity on her, she turned her head away as tears of inadequacy slid down her face onto the sheets.

One hand pressed her head persistently, making her look back at him, as his other one took her hand and slid it down his body until it reached the potency tenting his dress pants. Feeling him, so hot and hard and huge, made her whimper.

"That is how beautiful I find it, and you," he whispered.

Arousal overcoming distress, she twisted restlessly beneath him, moaning, "I don't even have words for how beautiful I find *you*. Please, Ivan, don't take it slow. Show me how much you want me, make me grateful I'm still alive."

His gaze filled with storms, but it was absolute care that filled his hands as he settled her back and slid down her body. Realizing what he intended, she was overcome by memories and, weirdly enough, embarrassment.

When she tried to keep her legs closed, he raised his head, his chiseled face flushed, his eyes coaxing. "Open yourself to me, Anastasia. Let *me* feast. Let me heal you."

"I'm healed," she cried out. "Please…"

"Your injuries, yes, but you're far from strong enough to withstand me."

The words *withstand me* unleashed a flood of memories, every sensation of every time he'd ridden her to screaming satisfaction. Though she was dying for him to do so now, to hold nothing back, she knew she wasn't ready for that.

"You can be gentle." She knew he could be, as he had been, heartbreakingly so, that first time he'd taken her. And every time, after their first explosive arousal had been assuaged, when he'd savored her in thorough, tender leisure.

But she saw it in his eyes. He had no intention of taking her that way. He came up to silence her protest before she uttered it, his mouth on her lips as his fingers sought her entrance. She lurched with stimulation as he dipped in, each slow inch a red-hot probe of mind-melting pleasure.

But though she was going to pieces with arousal,

after her trauma and after being so long without him, her body felt too tight. Even two of his long, thick fingers felt like too much. He held her eyes as he pumped them fully inside her, drawing the admission that there was no way she'd accommodate him right now.

Rising to singe her in the possessive flames of his gaze, he started sliding down her body again, burned his way in licks and nibbles and ragged words down to her core. Her efforts to pull him up ended when his magnificent head settled between her thighs. Every nerve in her body loosened as his lips and tongue soothed and scorched the intimate flesh she could surrender to no one but him.

He strummed her to one body- and soul-racking climax then another, and another, holding her eyes all through. She was lying stunned, sated, unable to move a muscle when he finally came up to stretch against her, cupping her, crooning to her, completing her bliss.

But she felt every inch of him like cabled steel, coiled on his unspent arousal. Needing to give him relief, she started stroking him, but he captured her hand. Burying kisses in her palm, he tucked her more securely against his massive body before taking her lips.

"Shh, *zvezda moya*." Murmuring another endearment into her mouth, my star this time, his tongue mated luxuriantly with hers. "I only want to hold you."

She moaned and burrowed deeper into him. "At least let me feel you. I need your flesh on mine."

His caresses stopped, then he rose partially, started shrugging off his clothes. As his body came into view, she realized she'd been right. He *had* become a full-fledged god.

Then she looked down on his promise of endless pleasure lying thick and long and heavy against his chiseled abdomen and nothing mattered but having him inside her.

She tried to wrap her legs around him in silent supplication, but he subdued her with extreme gentleness, wrapped his arms around her instead, letting every inch of his flesh imprint hers.

His lips flowed over her from neck to cheek, his whisper hot and soft against her prickling skin. "Let yourself take what I need to give you, *dorogoya moya*. Let go."

When she finally did, sank into his being and giving, the one thing left in her mind was that he was the only man who had ever made her feel this incredible, this protected and cherished. This man alone had the power to revive her. Or finish her.

Warm, wonderful sensations coasted over Anastasia, making her surface slowly from oblivion. Her eyes cracked open to light peeking between blackout curtains. Blinking, she expected to see herself back in her hospital suite.

In the next second it all came back to her. Everything that had happened since she'd come running home to see Ivan. Ivan, who was still stretched out against her, drenching her in caresses.

But maybe it had all been a dream, and still was. She'd seen and felt him like this on countless nights. And each time she'd woken up empty and alone.

"I'm here." As if he'd heard her unspoken question, he reassured her of his presence. He smoothed the hair off her cheek, tucking it behind her ear, the heartbreaking tenderness in his caress twisting her heart, spiking desire in her loins.

He'd taken her to bed at sunset. With the sun out again, she'd slept for at least twelve hours. Which might mean that...

He again completed her thought for her. "Your parents came to check on you. They were more than surprised to find me in bed with you." At her embarrassed gasp, something she hadn't seen since he'd come back played on his lips—the tiniest of smiles. "Don't worry, I'd already made us...decent."

It was only then she realized she was in a nightgown, her favorite one, a deep burgundy silk that felt like a second skin. He'd somehow picked it out of all her sleepwear and put her in it while she slept. He was fully dressed again.

"Did they...?"

"They just asked if you were okay. I assured them you were, and your mother insisted I have something to eat."

"Yeah, that's my mom for you. Though she is a scientist, the cure to everything in her opinion is a good meal."

"I ended up accepting tea and a huge slice of

delicious homemade apple pie. She served them to me right here."

Her cheeks flamed as she imagined that scenario. With her being a recluse, her parents had never had to deal with any man in her life. Her liaison with Ivan had been a secret, even from Alex. It had been the one thing she hadn't confided in him. And just as she'd thought it time to do so, Ivan had disappeared.

There'd been no one else since. It had been the main reason she'd never moved out of the family home. She'd had no personal life that she'd wanted privacy for.

Suddenly the indulgent gleam in his eyes dimmed, tension replacing it as he got out of bed.

He was going to say goodbye now.

She sat up, her heart suddenly thudding so hard she felt it rattling her whole body.

He looked breathtaking yet haggard. Longing almost stopped her pounding heart as his heavy-lidded gaze raked her, filled with disturbed and disturbing emotions. And she realized.

He didn't know how to say goodbye.

But neither did she. She couldn't say it. She needed him. In whatever way she could have him.

Not knowing how to tell him that, she rose on stiff legs, tried to postpone the inevitable. "You shouldn't have let me sleep all this time. And it doesn't seem you've had any sleep."

His jaw clenched. "Anastasia, we need to talk."

She groped for lightness, even though she was going to pieces. "That sounds ominous."

He clenched his fists, unclenched them. Then he squared his shoulders and stood straighter, as if he was readying himself for a frontal assault. "I tried, Anastasia. Tried to leave you alone, so you can restart your life. But you can't start again. Not yet. And I—I can't leave you."

Her heart did stop this time. Then it stumbled into a gallop of brutal anticipation. Did he mean…?

His next words ended all speculation. "Tell your family you need time to heal, which you do, and come with me." Before elation took hold, he added, "Let me do all I can to heal you."

The plummet from the heights of hope left her unable to breathe for long moments.

When she could finally draw breath, her voice was a rasp. "Is that what this is about? You feel responsible? Sorry for me? Guilty?"

He took an urgent step toward her, his eyes like emerald fire. "I sure as hell feel responsible. For your well-being. And I'm so sorry for what happened, I can barely breathe. And I feel so guilty it erodes my sanity. Guilty that I wasn't good enough or fast enough to prevent it. I want you to come with me so I can take care of you to my obsessive heart's content. But if you're asking if that's all, then no. I would want you with me without any of that. I've never stopped wanting you. I don't think I ever can."

Anastasia gaped up at him, this man she now needed more than life itself. Though he couldn't want her nearly as much, she believed he did want her, as much as he was capable of.

And he was right. She couldn't restart her life yet, couldn't resume her research without Alex, couldn't go back to the same place of work. He'd also been right to try to shield her from the world. It hurt even more being among her family now. And if there was anything she'd ever wanted, the one thing she'd been deprived of, it was being with Ivan.

His eyes seemed to seethe with anxiousness as he waited for her response. But before she gave it to him, she asked, "How long?"

"As long as it takes. As long as you want. Say yes."

Was there really any other answer?

"Yes."

His sharp inhalation said her acceptance took him by surprise. He'd actually expected her to refuse, or at least not to succumb right away.

"Don't you want to know where I'll take you?"

"It doesn't matter if I'm with you. If you want me…"

He gathered her to him, and she felt a tremor in those hands that were powerful enough to crush monsters. "I don't even have words for how much I do."

She fitted into his burning body, felt hers ignite. "Then I'll be with you, for as long as you do."

Five

A frisson of unease slithered down Anastasia's spine.

With a last look at her phone after she ended her latest call with her parents, who called almost every day, she exhaled.

It had been ten weeks to the day since she'd come with Ivan to Russia. And the ten-week mark didn't have a fond correlation in her mind. Not when it came to Ivan. It had been exactly ten weeks into their first relationship that he'd suddenly ended things. Just days before Alex and Cathy's wedding.

Not that she thought he was about to end it now. This time Ivan seemed bent on being with her, being there for her, for as long as she needed him. His constant dedication to her well-being seemed to be unlimited and unending. She had to continuously try to dial down his indulgence, pull him back from extravagant gestures. To generally convince him she no longer needed any special care.

And though he now let her do things for herself, and for both of them—cooking dinner had become her enthusiastic responsibility almost nightly— she kept learning what it meant to be with one of Russia's, and the world's, premier oligarchs.

Sure, she'd known he was a billionaire, had seen evidence of his wealth and power in so many ways, but the more she saw, the more it shocked her all over again.

Entering his mansion had been like stumbling into a level of existence she'd only dreamed of. She made—or had made—what she'd considered a very good living being a top researcher for an elite private conglomerate, had lived her life in her parents' million-dollar house, but this… This was just mind-boggling. His wealth had multiplied a hundredfold since she'd been with him in the past. And it made her…uncomfortable, feeling this unbridgeable gap between them.

This place alone cost forty million. When she'd said she'd never thought he would go for such extravagance, he'd confirmed that. He'd bought this baronial castle with its own lake, sweeping grounds replete with pine trees and a staggering forty thousand square feet of living space only after she'd agreed to come to Russia with him. So she'd have all the space and facilities to be entertained without leaving home.

He'd dropped forty million just so she didn't have to go out!

But she'd realized he'd been right. For weeks she'd been unable to contemplate being out in public, to see even strangers on the streets. The idea of meeting any of his acquaintances and interacting with them made her break out in cold sweat.

She had, however, insisted he go out alone. He'd refused. He'd locked himself up with her, so that he even worked across from her in the same room, or in the room he'd made into the nerve center of his cyber tech empire, running one of the major tentacles of Black Castle Enterprises right next to her favorite living room. Apart from the fleeting presence of Fyodor and his team of guards and hired help, Ivan had had no one for company but her.

He assured her he was a loner, with the only company he'd ever had in his life Dr. Balducci and his other partners. Even them he saw only sporadically since they were all so busy with their businesses and now with their families. And he insisted he didn't want anyone else's company but hers anyway.

But even if none of his assurances were to make her feel better, he couldn't enjoy being cooped up in the same place for that long, not even if it was acres wide. But her efforts to get him to go out met with dismal failure. He wouldn't budge from her side.

But for the past couple of weeks, she'd been feeling much better, regaining the desire to actually walk the streets and see people, and yesterday she had actually done it. He'd taken her on a tour of Moscow.

She'd been predictable and chosen to start with the famous attractions.

The whole morning yesterday had been spent visiting the *Krasnaya Ploshchad*, or Red Square, followed by the nearby and stunningly beautiful St. Basil's Cathedral, which exemplified Russian architecture. The two landmarks, now starting to get covered in snow, seemed to embody everything she'd ever imagined as Russian. The land she was born in but had never returned to, until now.

Today, it was the Kremlin's turn, where he'd made them jump queues and enter places no tourist was allowed, all through the five palaces, four cathedrals and the enclosing Kremlin Wall and Towers.

"Having a man of your influence for a guide obviously has its perks," she'd told him.

A teasing look had lit up his face as he'd winked at her. "You haven't seen anything yet."

She'd wondered what more there could possibly be as he'd taken them through a heavily guarded wing and into a massive, imposingly ornate office. It had only been when she'd found a man surrounded by half a dozen hulking bodyguards advancing eagerly to greet them that she'd realized what he'd meant, how accurate his words had been.

She *really* didn't remember everything that had happened in the time they'd spent in that man's company. A normal side effect, she was sure, of finding herself face-to-face with the President of the Russian Federation!

The meeting, an impromptu one that could only

have been planned at most the day before, lasted for half an hour. During the surreal time, both men had made her the focus of attention and conversation, with the president himself pouring her tea and asking her all kinds of courteous questions.

Then Ivan had said he was taking her to dinner and the president had stood up at once, asking Ivan for an extended one-on-one meeting. Instead of jumping to ask when, Ivan had actually given him an inconclusive answer.

Still stunned from that, and from the whole momentous event, she'd let Ivan sweep her out of the palace complex. Only now, when they'd been in his car for at least ten minutes, did she finally get over her shock enough to speak. She turned to him.

"Seriously? 'I'll see when I can clear a morning for you'? That's what you say when the second-most powerful man on earth asks you for a personal meeting?"

Keeping his eyes on the road as he negotiated Moscow's downtown traffic, he gave that lopsided smile that had been coming easier to him and that twisted everything inside her. "It's the only answer I had to give him."

"You direct your sprawling business empire from home these days, and you have the most efficient system humanly possible in place anyway. You can certainly 'clear a morning' at once for *the President of the Russian Federation* when he asks you to."

At a traffic light he slid her one of those heated glances that brought her blood to an instant boil.

"It's not only my business empire I have to take into account while clearing mornings."

"Seriously?" Her exclamation was almost a squeak this time. "You might have incurred the wrath of one of history's most powerful and dangerous men on *my* account?"

His lips spread wider at her burst of incredulous anxiety. "I'm too valuable to incur anyone's wrath. I'm also too dangerous that no one, not even him, would act on it even if I do."

Her heart drummed in rising apprehension. "C'mon, Ivan. Even you shouldn't risk putting that to the test, certainly not so you can babysit me. When will you believe I can spend time on my own and bring your obsession with watching me under control? For God's sake, I'm healed, fully, totally. Inside and out. *And* you have me ensconced in this fortress of yours with enough black ops guards to thwart a military invasion."

His gaze lengthened as he seemed to realize that her mortification was real. Then, putting the car in motion again when the light turned green, he pushed the hands-free button on the wheel.

In seconds the call connected and a voice she'd always recognize now emanated from the surround-sound system, answering in that heavily accented English. The president!

"Mr. Konstantinov, so good to hear from you again so soon."

Ivan's eyes briefly landed on her in an intimate caress. "You have Ms. Shepherd to thank for that,

Mr. President. She convinced me I could leave her side and come to meet you whenever you wish. You understand that with her recuperating from major surgery, her well-being comes first to me."

"I wouldn't have it any other way. I'll be only too happy to receive you whenever Ms. Shepherdova can spare your vigilant services."

Then with no closing words, both men hung up almost at the same moment.

Ivan turned those incredible emerald eyes to her, that indulgence that always filled them choking her up yet again. "Happy now?"

All tension drained from her body in a rush, making her slump back in the plush leather seat of his Rolls-Royce. "If you call feeling as if I've dodged a bullet happy, then yeah."

The smile froze over his magnificent face. "It really worried you that much?"

"Hello? I had a dozen scenarios scrambling my mind and in every one of them you were targeted for any level of disciplinary action!"

A frown crept over his face. "I wouldn't have arranged that meeting in the first place if I thought it would upset you. I wanted it to be a surprise you'd remember fondly."

"And boy, will I." At his darkening expression, she rushed on. "I *will* remember it in the best way, up until you offhandedly disregarded his request. Then it turned memorable for all the scary reasons."

At his stymied expression, she realized this was a

serious enough event she could use to settle the issue he'd been dodging since they'd come here at last.

Turning fully to him, she placed her hand over his arm, found his muscles bunched to the consistency of rock. "Want to know what upsets me? It's that you keep tailoring your every breath to what you think is best for me. That you won't believe me when I tell you what *that* is."

His jaw hardened, yet he made no response as he brought the car to a stop in front of what he'd told her on the way out of the Kremlin was one of Moscow's premier gourmet restaurants.

Before he got out to help her out, leaving the car to one of the guards who followed them everywhere at a discreet distance, he turned to her briefly. In the fleeting moments their eyes met, there was acknowledgment that he understood what she'd meant.

That he hadn't taken her yet.

Over the last ten weeks he'd exposed her to all kinds of intimacy and pleasure, brought her to dizzying heights in every way, except for the way she craved. He hadn't made love to her, hadn't claimed her, fully. By now she wondered if he ever would.

After she'd lost count of the times she'd begged him to take her, she'd stopped counting, and begging. She'd accepted from the start that being with him would be on his terms, that she needed him so completely, she'd take whatever he gave. Because at the time she'd made the decision, and even now, nothing at all from him wasn't an option.

But now that the ominous ten-week milestone was

here, his continuing resistance to act on his desire only made her suspect if it even existed. That this wasn't all some kind of debt he'd pledged to himself to pay, to her and to Alex. That would certainly explain his obsession with "healing her."

Yes, she had seen evidence of his desire, felt it, but now she wondered if it wasn't just the normal reaction of a virile male to an aroused female. Maybe, he thought making love to her that way came with too high a price, that of complicating his exit when he needed to walk away again. Maybe his desire wasn't strong enough for him to pay that price. Every day that passed made her a little readier to accept this explanation.

Feeling his mood had plunged as deeply as hers, she let him lead her into the restaurant in silence. The moment they entered, a tall, thin blond man, the maître d' presumably, came rushing toward them. A smile of eagerness broke through what looked like permanent disdain as he greeted Ivan.

As he led them inside at once, bypassing everyone who crowded the entrance waiting to be seated, every head turned to look at them. It was clear that most, if not all of the diners recognized Ivan, giving her a taste of what it meant to be in the company of a celebrity and under the microscope of public scrutiny.

Before they could be taken to the most exclusive table in the establishment that the maître d' had promised, half a dozen men and women stood up from a table in their path. Ivan stiffened as he saluted them without stopping, but they surrounded them, gushing in excitement over him and looking curiously at her.

Turned out they were waiting for Ivan to consider investing in their start-up. Having his ear in person was like a windfall they were ready to prostrate themselves for.

Realizing Ivan wouldn't give it to them, she turned to him and murmured for his ears only, "Apart from the president, it would be nice to meet live Russians who aren't your reverent employees."

His breath heated her neck as he whispered back, "You'll find those who wish for my favor are even worse sycophants than those already on my payroll."

But true to his ongoing quest to grant her every wish, he accepted the group's eager invitation to sit at their table.

Taking the plunge, she sat across the table for eight from Ivan, so that she could talk to others for a change. Not that there was much talking at first. It seemed the others were at a loss what to do with Ivan now that they'd gotten his attention. It was clear they'd expected him to turn down their invitation, had probably hoped at most for an invitation to call him directly. Now that he shockingly sat among them, they were as clearly overwhelmed by the godlike brooding entity who dominated the whole restaurant.

They grew more flustered when they ventured to speak, doing it in Russian, only to have Ivan answer in English. They tried to accommodate him, but none of them could hold more than a basic conversation in English. For some reason, Ivan never spoke Russian to her except in endearments though he knew she was fluent. She'd left Russia at only two, but her parents and Alex had continued to teach her. Wanting to put the others at ease, she spoke up in Russian, inviting everyone, starting with Ivan, to follow suit.

After that, to her surprise, being among a group of people, strangers but young and spirited, turned out to be far easier than she expected. It was an even nicer surprise to find herself falling back into the ease of her previously sociable self.

And all the time, she felt Ivan's gaze on her, even as he interacted with everyone, letting them court his favor but generally taking control of the gathering. And though he did it all smoothly, masterfully, every time one of the men had an aside with her, she felt a spike in the heat of his focus on her.

Basking in what she chose to label as jealousy, something she hadn't felt from Ivan before, she turned to the guy on her right. The man she was introduced to as Mikhail Popov was around her age with boyish blond good looks. He had been the funniest throughout dinner, and the easiest to read. His expression mixed blatant admiration of her with extreme awe and maybe a little envy of Ivan. More than a little tipsy now, he'd tapped her forearm to catch her attention. She turned to him and he stared at her blankly as if he'd forgotten what he'd wanted to say already.

Suddenly he blinked, then exclaimed, "Ah, yes. I heard that Mr. Konstantinov bought a mansion fit for a czar. Does it really have nine bedroom suites, two wine cellars and two indoor pools, not to mention thirty acres of gardens and grounds and a twenty-car garage?"

Anastasia smiled at his slurred, list-like question. "I haven't actually counted the suites, or the maximum occupancy of the garage, but that sounds about right."

Mikhail sat back in his chair, looking stupefied. "Now that's putting his money to good use, getting a place large enough to accommodate all of his mistresses at once."

His words fell on her like a kick, hitting her where she'd been shot, cut open and put back together. Not even the bullets or the post-operative wound had hurt that much.

To suppress her reaction, she turned blindly to yet another man who drew her attention on her other side. She didn't really hear what that other man said, didn't know what she said in answer, her stomach churning harder as she felt the intensity of Ivan's gaze flare up. She had no doubt he'd noticed her condition.

Then without preamble, he stood up and threw down his napkin, silencing everyone at the table at once, not to mention almost the whole restaurant.

He beckoned to the maître d', who came running, muttered instructions about settling everyone's bill. He walked around the table to her and her heart thudded at the barely leashed wrath in his predatory approach. For a moment she dreaded being alone with him. Yet to resist would probably cause a bigger scene than the one already unfolding, so she rose silently to her feet.

She wasn't sure if she managed an acceptable goodbye to their stunned and apprehensive companions, but she doubted they even noticed. They were too busy shivering at the malevolent glare Ivan turned on Mikhail. Ivan had noticed the blond man had been the one to upset her, and seemed to be calculating appropriate retribution. The poor drunk man probably had no idea what he'd said wrong, and most likely wouldn't even remember saying it at all when he sobered up.

Grabbing Ivan's arm, she tried to rush him away. She could have sooner moved a concrete pillar. As her nerves screamed in dread that he'd escalate right here and now, it seemed her mortification got to him. He suddenly turned his gaze to her, his eyes probing, solicitous. Taking advantage of his distraction, she tugged at him again and this time he let her steer him toward the entrance, where their coats and car were brought over.

The moment they were in the car, he insisted on knowing what Mikhail had said to upset her so much, but she managed to dodge his questions all the way back to his mansion.

Once inside, she tried to rush up to her suite, the one he didn't share. Whatever intimacies he'd been drowning her in, he'd always ended up leaving her to sleep alone.

As she started climbing the marble stairway to the upper level, he caught her hand.

"If you don't tell me what the man said, I'll have to go back and get it out of him myself."

She turned on him, her heart twisting in alarm, her voice sharpening. "You leave that poor guy alone."

"Not if he said something that disturbed you so much. Your face contorted as if what he said caused you physical pain."

How could he read her so accurately? And not at all at the same time?

It was she who gripped his hand now, needing to abort his aggression. "Promise me you won't go near him. Mikhail would probably drop dead of fright if you walked up to him and gave him one of those terrifying stares of yours."

"Tell me what he said!"

Wincing at his thundering demand, she let go of his hand as if it burned her. "He said nothing, okay? I just felt nauseous all of a sudden. It seems I didn't notice how much I ate while I was talking to so many people."

The muscles in his formidable jaw bunched, worked. "So that's the story you're coming up with to protect him. Now tell me the truth." When she only stared at him defiantly, he exhaled forcibly. "I promise I won't do anything to him if you tell me."

Hating to repeat Mikhail's words, furious with Ivan for trying to force her to, she stood her ground, took a challenging pose. "You'll promise you won't do anything to him regardless. And I don't have to tell you anything I don't want to."

Unable to chart his reaction, this man who expected obedience as his right, a moment passed in charged silence, as their gazes clashed.

Then, finally, she felt the tension gradually leave his tightly coiled body, the vicious fire in his eyes abating, until they were again the pools of cool emerald she now knew hid fathomless, roiling depths.

Finally conceding that she'd won, he sighed. "I won't do anything. And you never have to tell me anything you don't want to. But I'm asking you to please tell me. I can't bear knowing something hurt you, and I don't know what it is, how I can erase it, how I can stop it from hurting you ever again."

Reaching for her hands again, he pulled at her stiff body, brought her flush against him, letting her feel every inch of his hard perfection. Immediately the body he'd serviced and pleasured for ten long weeks wept for his ownership.

But because he hadn't really owned it yet, and with Mikhail's comment giving her fresh reasons why he hadn't, this time she resisted the need to succumb to him. The desire she'd been giving in to, willingly, breathlessly, since that day he'd taken her to her own bed, suddenly felt pathetic. She'd let it blind her to something that had always plagued their relationship, the prior one and this one, that she basically knew nothing about him. That nothing about the way he behaved with her made any sense. That with him, she couldn't form an opinion of the past, chart the present or predict the future.

But ever since he'd pulled her back from the brink of death, she'd accepted not knowing, had even told herself she didn't care to know so that she didn't have to make a decision or take a stand. But it ended now.

But Ivan's burning lips and hands were roaming her flesh, igniting her every inch against her best effort to resist. Before she could attempt to push away, he swallowed her protests, those hard yet lush lips mastering hers, his powerful tongue driving inside her mouth, filling her with the need to surrender again, to beg for him again.

But she couldn't do this again. Not if it meant a return to the status quo he'd imposed. Of him being so close, yet farther than the stars.

With an act of will she hadn't thought herself capable of, she tore her lips away from his sensual onslaught, pushed out of his embrace. It took him so much by surprise that he let her go so abruptly, making her stagger back.

After lunging forward to steady her, Ivan let her go. He looked down at her as if she'd slapped him.

Though she hated having to do this, after everything he'd done for her, she hardened her resolve. This was as much for him as for her. It was unfair to him if she continued taking advantage of his uncontrollable need to protect and indulge her. Not when it seemed to be at the expense of his own needs and life. He'd put everything on hold to be there for her, as he'd promised he would the moment she'd come out of anesthesia.

By now she knew he'd keep his word forever. As long as he believed she needed him he'd stay with her, be there for her in every way he could think of.

Except the way she really wanted and needed.

His inability to be with her fully, intimately, forced

her to face one possibility. That this was all for her, and there was nothing in it for him. And she couldn't do that to either of them.

Swallowing the rising tide of misery, she whispered, "I—I do want to tell you something."

His face lit up with a surge of eager supplication. "You know you can tell me anything."

"Can I?" Not finding the right words to say what stormed in her mind, she gave a nervous laugh. "I do tell you a lot of things, then you do what you unilaterally see fit anyway."

He started to protest, then stopped. There was no denying that he'd been overriding her. All for her own good in his opinion, but he'd done it nonetheless.

"But I am thankful you did it." She held up her hand to stop his usual protest. "And yes, you have to take my thanks. But it just has to stop, Ivan. You can't go on like this."

"I can, if you let me." Then, as if he heard his own words, he backpedaled. "But I promise I will pull back as much and as far as will make you comfortable."

"You're still making this all about me."

"It is all about you."

"No, it isn't, Ivan. There are two of us here. I suffered an ordeal, and you helped me through it. You were the only one I wanted help from. But time passed and my needs have changed and I no longer need that kind of help."

All light in his gaze was extinguished, making the ache she felt perpetually in her right side throb harder.

"Is this what you wanted to say to me? That you no longer want to be here?"

Her insides knotted tighter at the bleakness in his eyes, his voice. "I no longer want what you think is best for me. I want you to start considering yourself again."

"I am very much considering myself."

"No, you're not. And it's enough, Ivan. You've gone way beyond what I dreamed anyone could do for me. Now it's time for you to be with those you really want to be with."

His hands clenched at his sides, his whole body tensing. "What the hell is that supposed to mean?"

"Y-you know what I mean."

Suddenly something scary unfurled in the depths of his gaze. "This is about what Popov said to you, isn't it?" When her gaze wavered, unable to bear the brunt of his incensed one, he rasped, "Hell, Anastasia, just tell me what he said." When she hesitated, his eyes grew beseeching. "It was clearly about me and I have the right to know what it is, if only to tell you my side of it, whatever it is. I already promised you I wouldn't retaliate."

Knowing there was no way she could still hold out now that he'd put it that way, she reluctantly, haltingly told him.

"It was silly to react that way, but it did remind me that this artificial bubble you've created for me has nothing to do with your real life. You've interrupted it to come to my rescue, to stay by my side. But you now have to go back to your…"

She faltered as that terrifying thing in his eyes expanded, like a dragon unfolding its wings and preparing to spew fire.

It was more frightening that he sounded totally calm when he said, "That miserable piece of scum. I'll make him pay for that."

That had her pouncing on him, grabbing his arms in alarm. "No, Ivan, you promised."

His face looked again as demonic as it had when he'd been defending her and Alex, vanquishing their attackers. He gently unhooked her spastic fingers from his flesh, pulled away. "If I'd suspected he'd told you anything like that, I wouldn't have promised to spare him. This changes everything."

"No, Ivan, just let him be. It's not like he was trying to stir up trouble. What he said was the vodka talking. But then it's only expected for a man like you to have—" unable to say the word *mistresses* again, she just shrugged, her shoulders so taut they almost cramped "—you know."

That seemed to pour fuel on his terribly calm, and more terrifying for it, wrath. "A man like me? Do you or Popov or anyone else even think you know what kind of man I am? And it's only expected that I have mistresses? In the plural? At once? Do you think I have them all lurking around, on hold, while I play house with you? Or maybe I put you in bed at night and go make the rounds of my stable of kept women? Or worse, I have a harem all in one place as Popov suggested, to observe my convenience?"

"That isn't what I thought, Ivan, what upset—"

Her words choked off. Though there was much she didn't know about him, there were some things she was sure of. Beyond knowing that he had his own brand of unwavering integrity, he had this aloofness, this fastidiousness about him. What he'd just suggested, what translated Mikhail's comment in jarring detail, couldn't have any basis in fact.

She kept staring at him helplessly. Before she found the words to tell him her conclusion now, to beg his forgiveness for jumping to the wrong one before, Ivan's simmering gaze cooled down until self-reproach took over his expression.

"I'm sorry I overreacted." Though his voice remained as calm as before, it was now devoid of that dangerous viciousness, filling instead with entreaty. As she felt horrible that he was the one apologizing he made it even worse by adding, "I'll give Popov and his partners an in-depth interview to make up for the way I behaved tonight."

"That's great." She breathed in relief, glad for them, though it only made her more chagrined at how she'd behaved, how this had developed. "But I'm the one who overreacted, Ivan—"

His hand rose, interrupting her. "And you had every right to. You have no reason to trust me, Anastasia, with the way I left you in the past. What I do now doesn't erase it, doesn't exonerate me. I just never want you to be upset, never again, and certainly never on my account."

"Trust doesn't even factor into this, and it wasn't why I was upset. You had a life before you came

saving mine, and it would have been only natural if
you had—"

"I didn't, Anastasia. I had no mistresses."

"Please, just let this go, Ivan."

"No, Anastasia, I need you to know this. I had no
mistresses, in the plural or in the singular, not even
one-night-stands." His gaze lowered for a moment
before he raised it back to hers, showing her inside
him, the endlessness of his dark, tormented loneli-
ness. "I've had no one since you."

Six

Anastasia felt her heart, the whole world, grind to a halt. What Ivan had just said…

I've had no one since you.

The words sank in her mind, each one making no sense individually. Together they made even less sense.

She replayed them again and again, examining them for something she'd missed, or misunderstood. But there was nothing hidden or vague. He'd just said these words as clearly as could be.

He hadn't had sex with any other woman since her.

Then everything started to spin in a vortex of questions and confusions, a dozen hows and whys flying about around an epicenter of incredulity.

She felt as if everything inside her had been scat-

tered in disarray, her whole belief system and rational-
izations in shambles.

If he'd left her, but had never sought another... If
he'd kept an eye on her, but had never come back... If
he'd come back only in her extreme need, remained
with her, but still wouldn't be with her fully...

What did it all mean?

She stared up at him, lost in his solemn eyes. This
was too much, too unbelievable. She had to say something to do it all justice.

Then she opened her mouth and all that came out
was a blurted "No way!"

His eyes widened in astonishment. Then the seri-
ousness of his expression melted on the widest smile
she'd ever seen on his face, which was exactly what
her graceless exclamation deserved. To top it all off,
he treated her to another first. He threw his head
back and laughed.

It seemed laughing was such an alien activity to
him that it brought tears to his gorgeous eyes.

As his fit of mirth eased, he brought up both hands
to wipe his face. Then he looked at them, examining
the wetness in amazement. That only reinforced her
opinion that this had never happened to him before.
Or at least he'd thought it could never happen to him
again, for surely he'd laughed when he was younger.
A time she knew absolutely nothing about.

Her thoughts scattered when she suddenly found
him looking down at her as if he'd like to sink his
teeth into her and gobble her up whole.

Then he only said, "Yes way."

Her every inch started to burn again at the wickedly sensuous way he'd said that. And though it made her want to launch herself at him, tear at his clothes and beg him nonstop until he took her, she still had a million questions.

He continued to take her, do everything imaginable to her, with his eyes. But since she knew he wouldn't deliver on what those eyes promised, she quelled the pounding between her legs, tilted her head up. "And are you going to explain that?"

Scooping her effortlessly by her buttocks against his great body, he nuzzled her neck. "There's nothing to explain."

He felt so good she had to struggle to resist wrapping herself around him and begging him to take her right there on the stairs. She barely managed to pull herself away enough so she could look up into his eyes. "Oh, yeah? You drop a bomb of this magnitude on me—something that should be totally unbelievable— and you expect me to just take it in stride?"

Another of these frowns that always made her feel the sun had died gripped his face. "You don't believe me?"

"I said it *should* be unbelievable. Just the idea that a man like you would remain…celibate…" The word sounded so weird, so absurd. "For seven years! There has to be a big explanation for that. One you're not volunteering."

He eased her back on her feet, dropping his hands at his sides. "Again with this 'a man like me' thing. So let's have it. What kind of man do you think I am?"

Her cheeks blazed under his chilly gaze. "I don't think there are others like you for you to be a 'kind.' I only have theories from experience, backed up by the few facts you make available to the world. But really, when it comes to sex, any man wouldn't go seven years without it. And a man of your wealth and power, not to mention your looks and your…appetite, it's implausible you would."

"So you don't believe me." This time it was a statement.

"Of course I do." Her protest was vehement. It hadn't crossed her mind to question the truth of his statement. "I just don't understand how you didn't… why you didn't…"

He cut off her stammering, capturing her and raising her off the ground again and into his power, wrapping her thighs around his hips. "*You* didn't."

His surveillance of her had been that thorough?

But of course it had been. She doubted anything could be kept a secret from Ivan if he decided to uncover it. But it was still hard for her to accept that he'd found out what had gone on behind the closed doors of her life.

Suddenly, she wanted to call him out on it. At least, to challenge him. She'd made it too easy for him so far.

Arching backward, she let her long hair fall over his arms crossed over her back. "How can you be sure of that?"

The heat in his eyes rose, the hardness pressed between her legs becoming that of steel. "I'm sure. I've been watching you."

Another stab of arousal pierced her core, even as a chuckle burst on her lips. "And now I'll hear that song scoring your every move and glance."

The hands squeezed her buttocks harder, sending delicious electricity coursing through her. "What song?"

She locked her ankles more securely around him, her eyes getting heavy under the onslaught of hunger. "Y'know, The Police? 'Every Breath You Take'?" She sang the lyrics, somehow keeping in tune despite what he was doing to her. "Stalker much, Ivan?"

The flare of voracity in his eyes made her think that he would give in to desire this time, lower her right there and mount her. And oh, how she wanted him to. But then he let out a ragged breath and started walking up the stairs with her still in his arms.

"It would have been stalking only if I made you realize I was watching you." He paused a beat. "And I was watching Alex, too."

"Neither of us had a clue." Unable to let Alex's memory derail her current concern, she forced a smile. "But you've been watching me since you came back and no longer try to hide it."

"That's different." He grimaced as he shouldered open her bedroom door. "Or maybe it isn't that different." At the foot of her king-size bed, he bent and laid her with extreme gentleness on the turquoise satin quilt, what he'd said he'd picked to reflect her eyes, hovering over her with arms planted on both sides of her head. "If it bothers you, I'll stop."

She had two options. Surge up, clamp him with her arms and legs, bring him on top of her and risk a repeat of most nights since they'd come here, ending with her sated yet more frustrated than ever, and with this conversation aborted. Or resist the compulsion of his lure and her lust, and insist on getting answers. Once and for all.

She rose to her elbows, making him unfold to his full height. She almost swooned back again at the sight of him looming over her, oh so visibly aroused and crackling with hunger.

It was experience saying it would go nowhere that made her sit up. He kneeled in front of her, opening her legs and pressing between them. She knew that position by heart by now. According to him he'd become addicted to her taste. And at the first sign of weakening, he'd have her naked and in the throes of one orgasm after another. Like most nights he'd tire her out with too much pleasure. And then she'd wake up to find herself alone.

Not tonight. She pushed back against him when he tried to prostrate her in front of him. "Can you? Stop? I was just thinking that it has developed into some sort of obsession."

"No, it hasn't." He leaned back, so tall that even on his knees his eyes were level with hers, combed the luxurious ebony silk that had fallen over his forehead back in a self-deprecating move. "Developed, I mean. It has always been one."

"Why? Why did you do it? Why did you watch us all these years?"

Solemnity came into his eyes again, making them even more compelling. "Because I needed to make sure you were okay."

"And when you realized *I* wasn't, as evidenced by the fact that I couldn't move on, why didn't you do something about it? Wasn't that the whole point of watching me?"

His lips twisted on what looked like self-contempt. "I should have done something about it."

She fought the urge to catch those lips that had owned her every inch and pleasured her beyond coherence. "But you didn't. Want to tell me what stopped you?"

He lowered his eyes, escaping her beseeching ones. "Whatever it was, I should have found another way to be with you. It's yet another thing I will never forgive myself for."

Knowing she'd get no answer from him on this point, she tried another tack. "You only came back when our lives were at stake, so it's clear you wouldn't have come for anything less. So why didn't *you* move on?"

With each question he looked as if he would have preferred if she tore off his nails instead. But there was something else with this one. It was as if he'd never actually put the reason into words, even to himself.

Then he finally raised his eyes, and what she saw there almost knocked her flat on her back. "Because as long as you didn't find someone else, I considered that you were still with me."

A tremor started in her deepest recesses, one of searing, incredulous hope. "So if I'd moved on, you would have, too?"

"I very much doubt I would have. I had no way of finding out before I was with you, but I've since discovered that I'm monogamous."

He was monogamous. There'd be only one woman for him. Her.

This was too huge. Too…everything.

Unable to hold back anymore, she surged forward, hugged all she could of him in trembling arms. "You must be part wolf as I always suspected."

He kissed the top of her head, then dragged his lips against her hair, down her forehead, her cheeks. "It's very likely." He pulled back just enough to look into her eyes, and she saw the feral danger simmering in them. "But if you had moved on, I would have come back just to take that other man apart."

Delight swirled inside her at his possessiveness. "Now that's not wolf-like. That's pure dog-in-the-manger."

"I know. That sounds really messed up." His eyes sobered, making her almost cry out in dismay. She'd meant it teasingly. But it was clear he was ready with self-recriminations. Taking her arms off him in utmost care, he stood up. "It *is* messed up. *I* am."

Every nerve firing in alarm at the turn this conversation had suddenly taken, she scrambled up. "Is this what you really believe?"

He squeezed his nape in a punishing grip. "It's a fact."

She swept a hand across his chest, almost afraid he'd push it away. He didn't. Instead, he leaned into her touch as if he couldn't help himself, letting out a tortured groan.

Breath hitching with emotion, she unlocked his viselike hold on his neck and caressed it. "And does this fact have something to do with why you left, why you stayed away?"

"It does." An expression she'd never seen before, a tortured, defeated one, came into his eyes. "I thought you were better off not being anywhere near me."

She reached up and pressed a kiss on his stiffened lips, needing to absorb his distress. "And it didn't occur to you to let me have a say in what I thought was better for me?"

He growled in self-disgust and stepped away from her. "Just look what you did after I left you. You should have hated me, should have gotten over me. You didn't. We both know if I'd given you a choice, you would have wanted to be with me even if it destroyed you."

"You almost did anyway when you not only left me, but left me so suddenly and without an explanation."

His teeth made a grinding sound that made her wince, his eyes blazing like a cornered wolf's. "I wanted it to hurt, so you'd forget me. When I realized I hurt you *too* much for you to ever venture into another relationship, I took solace in the fact that you were at least safe and successful. And I told myself that you might still find someone."

Taking the opportunity to infuse a measure of lightness into the mood, she teased, "The someone you would have come back to take apart."

His eyes squeezed shut. "I already admitted I'm messed up."

She reached up to cup his face. "Well, I'm messed up, too, now, in case this is what's still stopping you."

"You're *nothing* like me, *moya dusha*." His hands covered hers over his face, his eyes full of so much emotions, it was dizzying. "You have no idea what I am."

"I got a pretty good idea since you came back." The shake of his head told her what she'd always suspected, that whatever she'd extrapolated, no matter how extravagant, wasn't even close. She caught his face again, pleading with everything inside her. "Then don't keep me in the dark any longer, Ivan. Don't push me away anymore. Tell me."

His eyes flared with such fierceness it made her gasp. Then he shook his head again, turned on his heel and headed for the balcony. And though it was already freezing out there, he threw the shutters open, as if he was escaping a fire.

Grabbing a thermal shawl off the back of the brocade couch by the balcony, Anastasia wrapped it around her shoulders and stepped out after him.

It was a crisp, clear night, the moon a waxing gibbous. The air was still, making the cold bearable. She watched him as he fisted his hands on the marble balustrade and tipped his head back as if he was gasping for breath.

He looked like a knight of old, silvered by the

moon, carved from the night, invincible, incomparable, yet weary from battle. As if to accentuate his reaction to her approach, the wind gusted suddenly. His body stiffened more as she neared him, as if it was cast in bronze, the only animate things about him his satin mane rioting around his leonine head and his clothes rustling around his imposing frame.

"Ivan, please."

He turned as the wind died down and the moonlight deposited glimmers in the emerald of his eyes. Stepping closer, mesmerized by his magnificence, she reached for one of the hands that had saved her, took it to her lips.

His growled protest and attempt to withdraw his hand made her cling to it, cover it in kisses. "Besides everything you've done for me, letting me in, letting me understand, would be the best gift I could ever be given. Give it to me, *please*."

Without warning, she tugged his hand. She hadn't even intended to do that. Surprise made him jerk forward the step that separated them, ending up pressed against her from breast to calf. Her hand released his, went to his head, sifting through the silky locks, bringing it down to hers, pressing her longing against his forehead with lips that shook on a litany of pleas.

His groan sounded as if it tore through all his vitals to rasp on his lips. "I can't, Anastasia. I *can't*."

Holding back tears, she let him go gradually, only so she wouldn't sag to the ground. "As you wish, Ivan. Like you said I have a right not to tell you anything I didn't want to, it goes the same way for you."

Turning on her heel, she walked back into the warm room, felt him following her, closing the balcony door behind him. She heard his breathing leveling out and she knew what would come next. He'd take her back in his arms, start to arouse her, worship her, give her everything he thought she needed, but the one thing she truly did. Himself.

And she couldn't take it anymore.

She *was* healed, was her old self again. Or maybe even a new self. One that couldn't drift in this realm of coddling and contradictory behavior and withheld explanations anymore. One that needed answers. Direction. Solid ground, whatever it was, to stand on.

The moment his hands landed on her shoulders, she whirled away. "I'm sorry I pushed, Ivan. But I don't need you to put me to bed. I can handle that on my own. I can handle giving myself pleasure, too. I've been doing it for years without you, after all. You also seem fine being without me, in the past and now."

His huffed laugh was vicious, bitter, as if he'd never heard anything so ironic.

But it no longer mattered what he felt, that he'd never wanted anyone but her. Not if he didn't act on it. And it was time to make him choose a path.

"I can accept that you can't trust me with your secrets—"

"It has nothing to do with trust, Anastasia." His objection was vehement. "I would trust you with my life and far more."

"Whatever your reasons, I can live with knowing only what you choose to reveal to me. You were right, about what I would have done had you given me a choice in the past. I would have wanted to be with you, no matter the price. Even now, without knowing what is so unspeakable about you or about the reasons you left me that you can't divulge, I still want you, Ivan. I *crave* you."

At his urgent step, she raised a hand to stop him from coming closer, afraid she'd settle for whatever he gave her if he touched her again. "But I can no longer accept this status quo you've imposed on us. I can no longer exist in this limbo." She paused, to brace herself for what she was about to say, to surmount the fear that when she did, it might end everything. Then she said it. "So it's up to you, like everything has ever been. But this time I get to give you a choice, Ivan. Either take me, or let me go."

Ivan's heart felt it might race itself to a standstill.

Anastasia wanted him. She'd been craving him from that first night. But tonight, with everything coming to a head, they'd come to an impasse. And her hunger was killing him.

All he wanted anymore was to snatch her up into his arms and plunder her like she'd been begging him to for the past ten weeks of torture.

But he hadn't taken her because he'd brought her here for her, not for him. Because he didn't want to make it any harder for her to walk away once she was fully healed, if that was what she felt was better for her. He knew he'd only drown her with him, like he had in the past. He'd been assuring that she had a way back, a way out.

Now she was giving him a choice.

Either take me or let me go.

He should let her go. She was healed. As much as she could be without the passage of time. There would always be echoes, throughout her life, moments when she choked up, when she was thrown back in time and into the middle of the ordeal. But her PTSD had been controlled, and she was as stable and strong as he'd hoped to get her. He should let her go so she could continue the part of getting better that only returning to her normal life, away from him and the rarefied environment he'd created for her, could achieve.

He *must* let her go. Even if her eyes pleaded with him not to. He had to draw on his reserves of strength, what he'd expended to keep away from her all these years, what had miraculously kept him from plundering her every time she breathed near him in the past weeks.

But he had no more strength. It had been long depleted. He'd been running on fumes, on prayers, on the sheer tendrils of sanity he had left. That was all he had to prevent him from dragging her deeper in with him, into his fathomless abyss of a soul, into the inescapable grasp of his passion.

But she wanted him to.

She had no idea what she was inviting.

But she didn't seem to care.

If he took her now, and then she changed her mind, could he let her go? Could he walk away again?

Did he even know how anymore?

As the debate raged in his tortured mind, her eyes squeezed tight, her whole face crumpling on despondence as she turned away, heading to the en suite bathroom.

He watched her walking away, one slow step after the other, as if she feared she'd shatter if she moved too fast.

He, too, was afraid to move, lest he let out the maelstrom raging inside him. Then he heard the shower running.

The images bombarded him. Of her stepping under the pummeling water, eyes closed and lips open, her silky, golden hair streaming down her back to her perfect buttocks, her healed, lush body gleaming, the water kissing it everywhere...

He wanted to stampede in there, feast on her, wrench pleasure from her depths, make her weep with satisfaction again.

But he knew she'd never succumb to his pleasuring again. She'd let the hunger gnaw her hollow before she did. For she didn't need release, she needed his possession, his dominance. She needed to lose herself in his passion, and sate herself with his invasion.

He felt the last tethers of his control snapping. They lashed about inside him, catapulting him after her.

She wanted him. She got him.

God help them both.

Seven

Ivan walked into the bathroom and his heart almost burst.

Anastasia was in the large shower stall, her back to him, leaning her forehead on the marble wall, as if the steaming jet beating down on her was almost too much for her to withstand. Without seeing her face, he knew she was weeping.

She hadn't wept in weeks now. She'd even started to talk about Alex without her eyes filling, without choking on the misery and finality of his loss. And he'd managed to take her back to that terrible place of vulnerability, where she felt so anguished and helpless. But he hadn't been able to tell her what he felt would only burden her more. Knowing his past would have been just one more scar for her to sustain.

But that wasn't the only reason. He had to be honest with himself. He feared she'd be horrified, repulsed, if she found out the truth about him.

His slow approach toward her suddenly stopped at a slam of realization. That this could have been the real reason he hadn't confronted her before he'd left her in the past. Maybe he'd dreaded if she'd known, she would feel relieved to be rid of such a monster, would have tried her best to forget him, to replace him.

Dog-in-the-manger, as she'd said.

He was more messed up than he had realized.

But even knowing so, there was nothing he could do about it now. Even if he overcame his own aversion to exposing the ugliness and madness in his past, telling her now would only disturb her more. And this he wouldn't do.

But if he couldn't satisfy her need to know, he could offer her what neither of them had been truly alive without. The all-consuming intimacy that they'd never be able to find with any other. At least he could give that to her for now. While she still wanted him. The man she thought he was.

His steps resumed as he started to unbutton his shirt. By the time he opened the shower, he was still clothed but he couldn't wait any longer to have his hands on her.

It all happened at once. He got drenched, she gasped at feeling his entry and he was wrapped around her, taking her from her slump against the wall back against his thundering body, into the shelter of his no longer containable passion.

She twisted around to face him with a cry, her eyes streaming with both water and tears, glittering with one unspoken question.

He answered it. "I can't let you go."

He tried to obliterate the distance she'd put between them but her trembling hands flattened against his soaked shirt, pain filling her eyes. "I can't have this be the only reason."

A self-deriding and loathing huff escaped him. "The one thing that stopped me from taking you was trying to do what was best for you. For me, holding back has been a hell second only to the years without you, to when I lost Alex and thought I'd lost you, too."

He thought, hoped, his confession would appease her, at least explain his behavior. But what she did next had him so stunned his heart forgot to beat.

Anastasia slapped him with all her strength.

That wasn't saying much, compared to the blows he'd sustained in his life. But from her, it brought him to his knees, figuratively, as he realized just how much he'd hurt her.

She glowered up at him through the jet of water, her enraged eyes the most beautiful and overpowering he'd ever seen them.

"That's for all these years of hell." Then both hands slammed on his chest, wet, sharp lashes of fury. "And that's a reminder to stop making unilateral decisions on my behalf." Next she pummeled him, as if she wanted to storm his being, to break down his barriers.

"And that's for driving me mad with your contradictions, with all the things you think you're protecting me from." Then her hands were knotted in his hair, bringing his face down to hers for an openmouthed, desperate kiss, her voice a hot tremolo breaching him to his very core. "And that's for saving me, for being the only one I'll ever crave. The absolute best and worst thing that has ever happened to me."

Before he could try to even think of how to deal with her lightning-fast mood changes, she pushed him away again, hands clawing at his shirt as if it was her worst enemy, tearing at the sodden material, ripping off the buttons he hadn't undone.

"And that's for coming in here still clothed," she panted as she attacked him, lips and teeth suckling and biting at every inch of flesh she'd exposed. "For making me wait again."

Everything that had ever held him back, every shred of control, every dread, every heartache, snapped, unleashing the longing and hunger that had been accumulating inside him.

Grabbing her hands, he pinned them above her head against the wet wall, while his other hand skimmed her lush curves greedily. But Anastasia wouldn't be held back anymore, squirmed to escape his hold, to continue exposing him to her hunger. He lasted only moments before he stopped her fumbling efforts and shredded the remainder of his clothes,

Shoving them away, he kneeled before her, looked up at her, this woman who embodied everything that mattered. As she sobbed his name over and over, he rubbed his lips, his whole face against her scar, the evidence that she'd survived, that he'd been given a second chance, one he'd almost wasted.

"Anastasia." He reiterated her name like a prayer, soul and body rioting with savage poignancy as he rose and lifted her off her feet.

As she crushed her swollen, hard-tipped breasts against his chest, rubbed her firm belly against his steel erection, he wrenched back at her lips. "No more waiting, *moya dusha*, never again."

He boosted her efforts to clamp her legs around his buttocks, fusing their lips as he flexed his hips until his erection nudged her entrance. He went blind with arousal as her hot, molten core scorched him, her face scrunching with extreme lust as she opened to him fully.

But as he began to ease himself inside her, she bit down hard on his lip. "I can't bear slow or gentle. Give me all you have, all your strength and greed. Devastate me. Finish me."

"Anastasia, *moye serdtse*..."

And she was his heart. He could have more easily withheld his next heartbeat than deny her what she needed. Holding her gaze, he thrust inside her, hard and fierce, invading her with the power they'd both been going mad for, stretching her beyond her limits. Her scream of agonized exultation tore through him as she consumed every inch of him in her clenching hunger.

At last, he thought, groaned, over and over. *At last*.

Incoherent with the pleasure, with the possession,

but still needing more, he filled his savage mouth and hands with her flesh, needing to plunder all that she was, leave no fiber of her being unclaimed. Her body yielded to his invasion while he watched greedily as wonder, pleasure and relief splashed across her magnificent face, squeezed out of her in splintered cries.

He'd filled her depths with that first ferocious plunge. He dropped his forehead to hers, overwhelmed, transfigured.

"At last, *moya dusha*..."

Her graceful back was a deep arch, letting him do it all to her. "Yes, Ivan, yes... I missed you, went insane missing you. Give me everything now. Ivan, please, now..."

Obeying her, he withdrew all the way out of her, roaring at the loss before ramming back into her tightness, that sheath of absolute ecstasy and oblivion that he'd craved until he'd become a shell of a man.

She was everything. The perfect fit, the end of his exile. Every glide inside her, the reality of their merging, the unimaginable pleasure of it, sent him straight out of his mind.

Her whimpers were delirious as her slick flesh clamped around his length with a force he was only too familiar with. He had craved it to the point of insanity throughout the years, and far beyond in the past weeks.

But she was tightening even more around him, contracting in forceful waves, her cries sharpening, getting more desperate, and he knew. She was already orgasming. She wanted him that fiercely, was that aroused, it had taken only a couple of thrusts to drive her over the edge. He pushed her hard over it and into an explosive climax, wrung her voluptuous body of every last drop of sensation and satisfaction.

He built the momentum of his thrusts all through her orgasm, until he was jackhammering inside her, until her whole body stiffened around him again, inside and out, absorbing all the ecstasy he rode her to. Her breath came in tortured keens as she hovered once more right at the edge of devastation. Then she exploded again in his arms. Her flesh rippled around him as bursts of completion convulsed through her, wrung him from the deepest point where he buried himself inside her, her screams stifling.

He withstood her storm as she expended every shudder and tear. Then he finished her as she'd always craved him to, impaling her beyond her limits, lodging himself at the gates of her womb and letting his own pleasure scorch through his length, filling her.

Her convulsions spiked at the first splash of his seed, sending him spiraling out of control along with her in the throes of a release that was the most powerful he'd ever experienced, even with her.

Plummeting into a realm where nothing existed beyond being merged with her, he rocked them together as they rode the aftershocks. All he knew was that he was still pouring himself into her, feeling her enveloping him inside and out.

Anastasia. His again.

It had been everything, beyond description. Yet

not enough. Nothing had ever been enough with her. He'd always wanted more, always would.

Unable to stand any longer, he sank down to the marble floor, barely aware of the water still raining down on them. Only she had ever made him powerless. Since he'd first seen her, she'd been his undoing. Now he wrapped himself around her, the woman who'd been made to take him whole, to fit within his arms and being.

He realized she'd gone limp in his arms only when she lurched, a gasp seeming to restart her breathing. Her eyes, slumberous and replete and adoring, snared him, ate him up whole, sending fire raging through him again. She was a goddess of temptation and benevolence and fulfillment, one he'd always felt unworthy of. It never ceased to humble him that she, miraculously, wanted no one but him. Gratitude and greed surged inside him, making him crush her against him as he drove all the way inside her again.

Her eyes squeezed shut as she gasped, her core contracting around his fully engorged erection, making him thrust deeper into her, wrenching moans from both of them. Her eyes snapped open, scorched him with the amalgam of pleasure and pain that intensified her one-of-a-kind beauty. She brought his face down to hers, merging their lips, too.

His mind was a total blank as his tongue mated with hers in a languid duel. Though he'd been kissing her almost nonstop through the past weeks, this was different. This was total, complete. Tasting her while holding back, he'd felt like Tantalus, unable to ever quench his thirst until he'd felt he'd shrivel up and expire. Drinking from her lips now that they were sharing their bodies in profound intimacy again was a revival. Even her name described what she was. A resurrection. His resurrection.

Soon the leisurely pleasure caught fire, and she was writhing in his arms as he pounded himself up inside her until they exploded simultaneously into an even fiercer, more prolonged orgasm.

An eternity later, he relinquished her mouth to gaze down at her. Her head fell back, her face drugged with satisfaction.

Then those lips he'd kissed swollen and deep red moved, and that beloved voice poured out in a heart-breakingly tender melody. "I want you again, Ivan. And again. I want to make up for all the time you wouldn't let me have you."

At her words he hardened again immediately. It was as if their previous two times served only to whet his appetite. As it always had. Whenever he'd taken her in a fury of haste, the explosive satisfaction had only left him wanting more, the kind of pleasure that only slow lovemaking would bring. And that had been when he'd been ignorant of one paramount fact. That no other woman would do.

Now that he knew every cell in his body was her personal property, no matter if she would have him or not, his desire frightened him with its magnitude.

But she did want him the same way. She wanted him with everything in her. For now. And for as long as he could have her total desire, he would give her his everything.

Adjusting her in his lap, over his erection, he began to move inside her again. He luxuriated in possessing her, in exploring her body and plumbing the depths of her responses as he loved her. He gave her two more screaming, heaving orgasms before he took his own roaring release.

After he'd rinsed and dried them both, he scooped her up and headed toward his bedroom this time, where he intended to keep her for as long as she would stay.

It was only when he was walking the huge corridor leading to his suite that she stirred in his arms, her question slurring. "Where are you taking me?"

He bent to kiss those swollen lips that could barely articulate words. "To my bed. Where I'll take you properly."

It sometimes seemed impossible.

Well, it always did, actually. That Ivan could give her even more pleasure every time he made love to her. But he did.

Ever since that day six weeks ago when he'd given in and given her himself totally, every time he took her, it was even better, more carnal, yet more profound. He'd been very eloquent and copious with expressing his passion. Far more poetic than this science nerd could ever be. He told her every time he touched her, it was like he tapped into another realm, where neither of them had limits, where the potential for pleasure and unity was infinite.

Anastasia sighed, stretched in bed, every cell buzzing with bliss as she watched Ivan through the open door of his gigantic bedroom, theirs now. He was coming into view then disappearing as he walked to and fro in the attached living room, his deep voice barely audible so as not to disturb her as he no doubt settled a business matter with a subordinate.

She'd never felt like this before, not even with him. Their rapport had been growing with every touch, every glance and word, as if the ordeals they'd endured together had somehow given each a direct link to the other's very essence. Now they were learning to perfect each channel of communication between them, every spark of sensation. The most incredible thing was his becoming that vocal in expressing his feelings, in communicating his thoughts and memories.

Not that he'd ever crossed some lines. He hadn't put a name to those feelings, or ever went back in time further than when he'd been establishing Black Castle Enterprises with his partners, whom she'd discovered were more than brothers to him. It had been okay with her, as she'd thought it was only a matter of time before he let her in all the way.

But that had proved the only blot in the perfection. That she by now believed he never would.

Suddenly, the bone-deep contentment of waking up in his bed evaporated. Getting up, she put on the turquoise silk robe he'd bought her, another thing that echoed her eyes, which he loved to see.

Walking to the balcony, she opened the blackout

curtains, let the cool late November daylight in, looking over the sprawling, snow-covered grounds, trying to shake off the dip in her mood.

She was being too silly, too greedy, needing to reach as deep inside him as he had inside her. But she had to live with the fact that there was far more to him than there was to her. Or anyone else for that matter. What had made him this incomparable man that he was had to have been experiences and tests that she couldn't even imagine. No doubt things he wanted to forget, might even regret. If he couldn't let her in that far, probably thinking she couldn't handle it, it shouldn't bother her. That it did was her own problem, not his. A problem she should deal with, once and for all.

"Did I wake you up?"

She whirled around at Ivan's vocal caress. She'd been engaged in such a struggle with her wayward thoughts that she hadn't heard his approach. He was behind her, then around her, encompassing her in his cherishing power.

She met his heated smile with her own. "I just woke up because you were no longer beside me."

"Now I am, and it's the only place I ever want to be." His breath flayed her lips, hot, virile, filling her lungs and being. "No one should wake up this beautiful. No one should be this beautiful, period."

Starting to tremble with that urgency for him that never abated, she ground herself against his hardness. "Look who's talking."

He pressed her back against the French window,

driving one pant-clad powerful thigh between her quivering legs where her robe opened to expose them. "Tell me, Anastasia."

He always urged her to tell him everything she was thinking, everything she wanted. It was as if he needed access to her very soul, to her every whim and need so he could satisfy them. Which he did. Apart from that one huge part of himself he never let her near, he was giving her everything there was to give. While she held nothing back from him.

Now she gave him what he asked for, full capitulation. "I find everything about you painfully, *distressingly*, beautiful." To accentuate her admission, she slipped her arms from around his neck, pushed his open shirt farther apart and covered the perfection of his chest in compulsive kisses. "Every inch of you, every move and word and touch, every callus and scar… It all delights me, drives me out of my mind, even more the more I'm exposed to you, the more I have of you."

His gratification—especially when she mentioned calluses and scars, which must be trophies of that blacked-out time in his past—was so ferocious it burned her. Though it had always disturbed her to formulate theories how he'd acquired them, tracing them with her fingertips and lips, feeling them raking against her skin, had always sent her clear out of her mind with lust. She found them as arousing and beautiful, awe-inspiring as every other part of him.

He ran his fingertips down her arms, slowly, tantalizingly, until they reached her hands, and he untangled them from his shirt. Then giving her such a wicked glance, he turned away from her. She watched him sit down on the couch facing the balcony, amazed all over again how the fever of anticipation and urgency only increased with every sexual encounter. Her heart shook her as he sprawled back, spreading his great body for her to drool over.

Then he beckoned. "Show me, *moya dusha*."

She called on all her self-control not to run to him but rather play the game of slow seduction he seemed to want. She undulated toward him, conscious of the robe slipping off one shoulder, exposing a generous swell of one engorged breast, and the effect that had on him. Black pupils ate up the emerald of his eyes, the rock hardness tenting his pants expanded, and the smoldering smile became purely predatory. Prolonging the moment and reveling in her ability to arouse him always and completely, she took her time to reach him.

But once her knees bumped his, she lost the fight. She collapsed over him under the weight of the seven years of unremitting craving she'd only started expending. Slowing her descent with shaking hands against his unyielding shoulders, she straddled his hips, her robe riding up her thighs. His eyes burned into hers with smug satisfaction until her lips crashed down on his.

He opened his mouth to her urgency, let her show him how much she needed everything he had. And she did. Her hands roamed his Herculean chest, his granite abdomen, until they reached his massive manhood, as she lowered herself to press her drenched core against it.

"I want you, Ivan. You just breathe, *I* just breathe, and I want you. All of you." She reached for his belt buckle, eager to unsheathe the formidable length of him.

At her feverish moans he stopped her uncoordinated efforts. Sighing in ragged relief, she let him take the lead, luxuriated in his domination, what he'd so maddeningly made her work for.

His hands roved her curves, pushing the robe off her burning body, his every move loaded with the ruthlessness of a starving predator unleashed on a prey long kept out of reach. It didn't matter that he'd spent the night feasting on her. Their fire consumed them only to rage higher.

His pupils flared and subsided, giving his eyes the illusion of flashing emerald. Then he bent to the breasts he was kneading, grazed and suckled her peaked nipples until he had her writhing, her breath fracturing, her arousal soaking his pants. After his devastating homage, he swept her around, spreading her naked on the couch. Opening her thighs wide, he took them over his shoulders as he came down on his knees between them. Before she could mutter a protest, he buried his lips in her flowing readiness. She shrieked at the feel of his tongue and teeth, opening herself fully to give him total access to her intimate flesh, what had always been his.

Then he nipped her bud, and the slam of pleasure told her that one more suckle or graze would finish her. And she didn't want release this way, even if she knew he was addicted to giving it to her. She was addicted to *him*, to merging with him, feeling his potency invade her, fill her every emptiness and loss and need.

"Ivan," she gasped. "I need you inside me."

Growling, he heaved up, caught her plea in his savage mouth, sharing her taste on his tongue. In one fluid motion he rose, lifting her in his arms. But instead of taking her to their bed, he took only a few steps before he stopped abruptly, pressed her with her steaming back against the cool, smooth wall. Capturing her there with his massive body, he locked her feet around his buttocks, thrilling her again with his strength. Then he leaned back, freeing his erection.

As always, the potency she'd worshipped so many times, that had possessed her during so many long, devastating rides to ecstasy, had her mouth watering, her core clenching. The intimidating weight and length of it thudded against her swollen flesh, squeezing another plea from her depths. He glided his incredible heat and hardness through her molten lips, sending a million arrows of pleasure to her womb. But he didn't penetrate her until she cried out.

"*Fill* me."

Only then did he ram inside her. Pleasure burst from every nerve ending at his carnal invasion. She was addicted to this, the first almost unbearable expansion as he stretched her beyond her limits around his length and girth. It was always a shock so acute, so exquisite, her senses flickered.

"Every single time, *moye serdtse*, you feel even better," he growled. "Anastasia…if only I could devour you whole for real." And it felt he tried to, his teeth sinking into her shoulder like a wolf tethering his mate in the throes of a feral copulation. Then he withdrew.

It felt as if he was dragging her life force out with him. Her arms tightened around his back, her hands clawed it, begging his return. He complied with a harder, deeper plunge until he forced her flesh to yield fully to him. Only when he'd breached her to her very core did he quicken his tempo. Every withdrawal was a maddening loss, every plunge excruciating ecstasy. In her heightened state she was aware of every sound and scent and sensation. Her cries that blended with her muttered name on his lips… The carnal sounds of their flesh slapping together… The musky scent of sex and abandon… The glide and burn of his hard flesh inside her. They all combined to rocket her to the point of combustion.

When she couldn't bear it anymore, he gave her what she needed, as he always knew just when, how hard and fast. He hammered between her splayed thighs, his erection pounding inside her with the perfect cadence and force to unleash everything inside her. She shattered in his arms.

Sensations radiated from the pinpoint of insanity where he was buried deepest. Currents of release crashed through her, squeezing her intimate muscles around him, drawing out every jolt of pleasure from her every inch. She felt him everywhere, igniting her every nerve ending, invading her heart.

Knowing he'd inundated her with satisfaction, knowing she now needed his, and his total domination, he roared her name and exploded in his own climax. With one last plunge he filled her to overflowing, sharpening the throes of her release. She felt him pulse the last of his seed into her depths, completion imbuing her as she slumped over his chest…

A rumble beneath her ear jogged her back to consciousness. "Perfection, Anastasia. Every single time. And more."

Feeling boneless, she tried to nod her spinning head in agreement as he carried her and started walking, still buried within her depths. Knowing he'd carry her to bed now, she drifted off again.

Jerking out of her sensual stupor as he laid her down, she twisted around sensuously in the cotton sheets imprinted with his scent and that of their intimacy, compensating her for his loss as he left her body to strip fully.

Coming back to her, he gave her his full weight, which she always begged him for after the storm, his heartbeat a slow thunder against her decelerating one, completing the spell.

She was drifting off when he rose off her, dragging a crisp sheet over her cooling, enervated body. She tried to rouse herself, and he spread soothing kisses over her brow.

"Sleep a while, *moya dorogoya*. I exhausted you and now I must refuel you."

Knowing he'd get them breakfast, she sank back in his indulgence and the echoes of his scent and passion.

Ivan took his time preparing breakfast, to let Anastasia rest. He really shouldn't have taken her twice in a row like that, after a night when he'd done it three times. His insatiable need for her frightened him at times. But at least it only seemed to delight her. She was always hungering for everything he could give her. And he gave her way too much at times.

He now walked back into their bedroom with a tray laden with everything she loved. His lips spread, remembering her accusing him of having a nefarious plot to fatten her up. He'd admitted he would enjoy having more of her to fill his arms, to fondle and squeeze and worship.

Not that he didn't find her perfect no matter her weight. But it was such a relief that after weeks of escalating delight in each other's company, her appetite had returned. She was also back to exercising and had never been more, as she'd said earlier of him, painfully, distressingly beautiful.

Placing the tray down on the bedside table, he luxuriated in watching her sleep off their latest lovemaking. Her lush body was tangled in sheets the color of her hair. Her thick lashes fanned her softly flushed cheeks, her lips swollen with his passion and her wild locks strewn over his pillow.

Suddenly, a white-hot spasm stabbed his gut as images of her bathed in her own blood and Alex's tore into his mind. Seeing her that way now, the image of health and contentment, had emotions raging through him. Every violent emotion, sublime and searing collided inside him, buckling his knees. He sank down on the mattress, a shaking hand reaching out to touch her, to assure himself all over again that this was the reality, that he had her with him, safe and whole and happy.

Her eyes fluttered open, absolute welcome and joy filling them at once. He forced himself to breathe, struggling to banish the brutal images that assailed him regularly back into the deepest dungeon of his memory.

Stretching and yawning delightedly, she sat up, looking like a goddess of voluptuousness, her breasts full and firm, her waist nipped, her thighs long and sleek, her hair gleaming gold around her strong shoulders. His body roared all over again. He tamped it down as viciously. It was enough he'd been all over her the moment he'd found her awake, not even giving her a chance to freshen up or eat. He really had to do something about his perpetual arousal, the need to possess her as many times as she could withstand every single day. He shouldn't unleash seven years' worth of deprivation on her. Even if she was breathlessly willing.

But she was now getting on her hands and knees, slinking toward him like a mischievous cat, rubbing against him very much like one, before turning all human female, pressing her softness into his hardness, turning his arousal to distress.

Pushing him on his back, she lay on top of him, pressing her every hot inch to his. "It's *you* I want to feast on."

He gazed up at her, needing to tell her so much, yet still unable to, the unuttered confessions a constant burning coal in his throat. "I'll be right here after you eat. I'll always be there for you to take your fill of me."

Next moment, her response made him like everything had come crashing down.

Wrapping one lock of the hair he'd grown longer as per her request, her smile inexorable seduction, she asked, "Always? Even when I go back home?"

Eight

Anastasia could no longer keep the knowledge from herself.

Not that she'd really kept it hidden. It was just she hadn't given her all-encompassing, overwhelming emotions for Ivan a name, not since he'd come back. But it had been a constant in her life, even when she'd thought he'd left her forever.

She loved him. Had always and would always love him.

But though he behaved as if he loved her as passionately, as absolutely, and was profuse with extravagant actions and endearments, he never put his emotions into those words. So neither had she. And in spite of everything he'd done, everything they'd shared, she dreaded that he'd one day suddenly end it again.

And that wasn't another attack of anxiety or paranoia. She had reason to think what she did. It had started that morning two weeks ago, when she'd introduced the subject of going home.

He hadn't answered her, had done it smoothly, heaving up to engulf her in kisses and coddling, feeding her breakfast before making love to her again.

He'd expertly avoided the subject since, diverting the conversation each time she tried to take it there.

By now she knew if she left it up to him, she'd never go home.

Though he'd been struggling not to show it, he'd been on edge, anticipating that his evasive tactics would soon run out, and they'd have a confrontation. She feared that when that happened, this rarefied state they'd been living in would come to an end. And this time, he *would* let her go.

Just minutes ago, she'd reached critical mass. She couldn't go one more hour without finally having this out.

Her footsteps faltered outside his office before she came into his view. He always left the door open, as if perpetually afraid she'd need him and he wouldn't be aware of it at once.

She inhaled one last bolstering breath and walked in.

His eyes flashed that all-out welcome at her sight. He rose at once from his massive mahogany desk with the multiple computer screens at his back. But his eager steps slowed down when he saw her face clearly. She was sure she looked as tense as she felt.

The momentary slowing turned into urgent strides that had him catching her by her shoulders in an anxious grip in seconds. "What is it, *moya dorogoya*? You're not feeling okay?"

Gripping his hands she tried to stem his anxiety, what could soar at the slightest provocation. "I'm fine, really. Don't start worrying. I just…wanted to talk to you."

His face emptied. But in the blankness she could see one important fact. He knew what she was going to talk about. And if he could have done anything to stop her, he would have. But she'd cornered him this time, and he could do nothing to escape the subject. And he hated it.

It made her almost back down. How she hated to force this confrontation, too. But it had to come, sooner or later. And now she knew it would, she could no longer postpone it and live in this progressively debilitating suspense.

Gathering all her strength of will, trembling inside in apprehension at the possible outcome, she said, "I've tried to bring it up before, but you clearly weren't ready to discuss it. I let it go as long as I could, Ivan, I really did. But I can't do it anymore. Even after what happened, the condition I was in when I first came with you, being with you here has been the most magical time of my life. But…"

His hands caught her arms again. "There shouldn't be any *buts*. It is magic, being together. And I never want anything to break the spell."

"I've thought about it long and hard from every

angle, and now that I'm healed, inside and out as much as I ever will be, I've changed my mind. I won't sit back and let you pull strings to honor Alex's memory. *I* will do that. I owe it to him, to our parents and to Cathy and the kids. I owe it to myself. Only then can I get closure and change my path."

His jaw muscles bunched, but he finally nodded. "Very well. If you will let me orchestrate this to the best outcome, you can be the one to make the final steps and announcements."

Grabbing his hand, she planted a fervent kiss in his palm. "Thank you…" He started to protest and a finger on his lips silenced him. "Just let me thank you, Ivan, please. I need to give you my thanks far more than you hate receiving it."

He gave another reluctant nod, before his eyes lightened, as if with relief. "If this is why you want to go back…"

She had to stop him. "No, it isn't. I do have a life back in the States, Ivan, a life I want to go back to. But I need you to tell me what going back would mean for us. I know you thrive on solitude, but I don't. I needed it for a while, to regain myself and my stability. But I can't continue being with you in such isolation from the rest of the world."

"Why not? It has been perfect that way."

"It has been more than perfect, but it has also been like a pocket universe, an alternate reality. We can't exist in this bubble forever. You have friends who're as close as family to you, and I do have a family. Two families."

At her last words, something dark and terrible filled his gaze. Something elemental. Bleakness? Revulsion? Even despair?

When families had been mentioned at the beginning of their relationship in the past, he'd only said he was orphan, adopted and abandoned again at an early age. It had been her cue never to mention family to him again, avoiding mention of her own in deference to his sensitivities.

But did it go beyond sensitivity? Did the scars of his childhood go way deeper than what she'd ever estimated? Did he abhor the idea of family, especially one that would invade his life, as hers would, through her?

If this was true, where would this leave them?

Heart pounding with trepidation, she ventured a direct gaze into those grim eyes and broached the subject that had been an unspoken taboo between them. "I realize family isn't something you consider kindly, and rightfully so, but my experience with family is nothing like yours. I—I love my family. I need them."

The sheer pain that came into his eyes made her hate herself for causing it. His next words, forlorn and agonized, hit her even harder.

"I thought you needed me."

"I do. Oh, God, I do. But needing them, too, wouldn't make me need you any less, wouldn't interfere in our relationship."

His whole face twisted as if unbearable bitterness

had just flooded his mouth. "It will. And I can't abide something coming between us."

Dreading his answer, she knew she could no longer dance around the subject, had to ask him pointblank.

"What will you do if—*when*—I go back to my life, the life that includes my family? Will you disappear again?"

This time he said nothing, his silent rejection far harsher than if he'd spoken it. A dozen emotions seethed in his eyes as they fixed on hers. It felt as if he was trying to bend her to his will, to make her relinquish this intention. And she had to face what she'd long avoided facing.

Ivan was incapable of leading a life among others. He was the wolf she'd once jokingly accused him of being. A lone wolf. If she wanted to be his mate, it would be either him or the rest of the world.

But though it would have been a terrible choice, knowing the nature of his scars, she *would* have chosen him over anything. *If* she didn't fear his inexplicable moods, what stemmed from his unknown and not-to-be-known past. If she didn't dread his future abandonment.

But there was so much she didn't know about him, and about the reasons he'd left her in the past. With so many things she couldn't understand about him, so much he hid from her, she couldn't bet her heart, her life and future on him.

It felt as if her heart broke for real, and, her chest was tightening over its jagged pieces, until she couldn't stop herself from crying out with the pain.

Her desperation released some shackle that had been holding him back and he caught her in a fierce embrace.

"Don't leave, *moya dusha*. Don't leave me."

She sobbed her desolation. "I never want to leave you. But I can't remain here where I have no life outside of you."

"Then I'll make you a life. Anything you want."

"I only ever wanted you. Going back doesn't make this any less true. It's you who's putting an impossible condition on being with you. You don't have to be involved with my family in any way if you don't want, but you can't expect me to just cut them off, too. You don't have to come back *with* me. Just say you will be back *for* me."

Again, his oppressive, horrible silence in the face of her entreaty, where all doubts mushroomed, shrieked for her to cut her losses. To go now, before leaving him became impossible, or even worse, before nothing much of her survived leaving him.

Feeling like she was reaching inside her chest and ripping her shattered heart out, her shaking hands undid his grip on her arms. "I want to go back to the States now, please, Ivan. You are free, as always, to do what's best for yourself."

Ivan had done what Anastasia had asked him.

He'd taken her back to the States. He'd insisted he'd be the one to drive her to her parents' doorstep, even when she'd tried to convince him Fyodor had better do it.

She hadn't wanted him to come with her in the first place. Extending the goodbye for all these hours, and up until these last moments, had been brutal, for both of them.

But he couldn't let her out of his sight before he saw her safe inside her family home. Only his over-powering reluctance now let her walk to their door on her own, rolling the single suitcase she'd packed from the innumerable things he'd bought her.

He sat in the car watching her go, paralyzed, unable to move a muscle or make a sound to stop her.

Knowing he *shouldn't* stop her.

All he could do was cling to her every nuance as she rummaged shakily for her house keys. She hadn't told her parents she was coming home, didn't even ring the bell. She probably didn't want to hurt him with the sight of her family receiving her in tearful welcome, when she thought his hang-ups stemmed from having no family of his own.

Her consideration tore at him all over again, her every move as she fumbled to open the door more slashes to his bleeding psyche. Then without a last look, she stumbled in and closed the door.

The moment she did, Ivan felt his heart being crushed. Literally. What else explained that stab that sank into his heart, making him lurch forward, his head shaking on the steering wheel and his lungs tightening on what felt like broken glass?

Giving in to the agony, he almost wished that it was a real heart attack, and that it wouldn't spare him. Almost. He couldn't wish for his life to end as long as Anastasia existed. As long as she needed him. As he knew she did.

But she needed more than him to complete her healing. She needed to resume her life. He'd tried to put that moment off for as long as he could, plying all his diversion tactics to postpone it. But even before she'd confronted him yesterday he'd already known. If he loved her, he should let her go.

And *how* he loved her.

He'd long admitted to himself that the all-consuming feeling that had blossomed into life from their first meeting and had only intensified as he'd gotten to know her, was love.

No. Far more than love. He now fully knew what his brothers, Antonio, Rafael, Raiden and Numair, even Richard, felt for their soul mates. This absolute admiration and allegiance, this endless desire and devotion. And he wanted with her what they had with them.

Union, children, permanence. Everything.

But that also meant being in extreme proximity with his own family, since they were a close and constant part of her life.

In her efforts to convince him that going back home, reentering her family's life wouldn't impact him or their relationship, she'd as good as pledged he didn't have to see any of them. But he knew this was impossible. How could he make her live in this abnormal state, torn between him and those who'd raised her? How could he force her to split herself in two, part for him and part for them, keeping the two halves separate, with her contentment lost in the middle?

He couldn't. He'd taken her away knowing it was best for her. He shouldn't have pressured her to remain in isolation with him the moment he'd realized it was no longer the case.

And now she was here. Back among the only people in the world he couldn't bear being around. The ones he had to abide if he wanted to be with her again.

Suddenly, the talons that had sunk in his heart retracted, letting him breathe. Because something was becoming clear.

Right now his agony was only over the idea of separation from her. None of his misery in these past hours had been about the aversion that had ruled his life since he was twelve. None of it had anything at all to do with his family.

Even if the dread of being around them wasn't gone, it was *nothing* compared to the unimaginable desolation of being without Anastasia. The idea of putting up with their presence in his life for as long as they lived, of even developing a relationship with them for her sake, wasn't abhorrent anymore. It even bordered on being welcome. As long as it made her whole and serene, as long as it afforded him the miracle of her presence in his life.

He had no idea if she even loved him a fraction of how he loved her. But that, too, didn't matter. Whatever she felt for him now was more than enough.

For a second chance with her, this time for life, he was willing, eager, *happy*, to put up with anything.

He couldn't believe he hadn't figured this out before.

Starting the car, he put it in reverse and backed up into her parents' driveway, in the exact same place he'd parked that first day he'd asked her to go with him.

This time, he would ask her to *be* with him. Forever.

Within ten minutes of being with her parents, Anastasia had expended all the hugs and kisses and the delight of seeing them again. Now an awkward silence descended on them. She really had nothing to say to them.

It wasn't only Alex's loss that gaped between them like a black hole that would forever suck any real brightness out of their relationship. They truly had nothing new to say to each other. They'd been talking regularly while she'd been in Russia, with her keeping them updated about her health while they'd kept her up-to-date with the incidents of their own uneventful lives, and the more bumpy adjustments of Cathy's and the kids'. She knew her mother and father had always itched to learn the details of her situation with Ivan—what she'd adamantly refused to discuss.

Now there was nothing to discuss anymore.

Ivan had succumbed to her desire to return home, had been immovable about delivering her here himself. As he had that time when he'd gotten her and Alex home. It had been almost as horrible as those dark days, sitting onboard his jet with him, knowing that the hours had been counting down to separation from him once again. This time for what looked like a final time.

Suddenly, it all hit her.

This could *actually* be the end.

And there was absolutely no way she could let it be that.

She heaved up to her feet so suddenly she made her parents exclaim in alarm. Excusing herself, she told them she had to do something urgently and would be in touch as soon as she could. Then she ran out of the room with them gaping after her.

She couldn't let Ivan go. She wouldn't. Not this time.

In the past, in Russia, she hadn't fought for him, for them. This time she would. Until her last breath, if need be.

Getting her phone out, she dialed his number as she ran to the door. And the phone rang. Not her phone. A phone on the other side of the door. For a second it didn't make sense.

Then she snatched the door open.

He was there, one hand poised on the doorbell, the other reaching for the phone still ringing in his pocket.

Their gazes collided, a thousand volts of longing and relief arcing across the distance between them.

Then there was none, both hurtling to obliterate it.

She flew into his arms. The home that was hers alone, the man who was her haven, her succor.

Her everything.

Ivan kissed her, devoured her, gulping air through her lips as if he'd been suffocating without her, as she had without him in that short time they'd been apart.

As if he, too, had felt his world coming to an end at the thought of losing her.

With tears flowing down her cheeks, she tore from his crushing embrace, needing to tell him everything she would do for him, for them. She grabbed his hand, dragged him behind her toward his car. Midway, she rethought her plan and doubled back toward the house, and up to her quarters, with Ivan rushing after her with his face an adorable mix of perplexity and compliance.

Closing the door of her bedroom, she tackled him down on her bed and stormed him with kisses, tears and smiles.

Then she realized something. Though he was surrendering to her, kissing her back with the same fervor, with the same shaky need for reconnection, that stiffness had reentered his body. Though he'd been unable to stay away, he was still loath to be there.

Putting this matter to rest once and for all was the one thing that could make her stop kissing him now. Pulling back, she was struck by the magnificent sight he made sprawled there, dwarfing the bed, the whole room, his raven hair strewn around his majestic head.

She opened her mouth to speak, but he spoke first, his voice hushed like a fervent prayer. But it was what he said that made her jackknife up, gape down on him.

"Anastasia, *moye serdtse, ya nye magu zhit' byes tyeba.* I can't live without you, my heart. I won't. Marry me."

His words and their meaning registered at once this time. And so did their total shock. He…he…

Ivan was proposing.

And she only knew one thing. She had to find her voice, to blurt out an acceptance.

But something held her back. His agitation. It went beyond worrying about her response. It hit pause on her surging jubilation.

She pulled him up. "There's something wrong here, Ivan. You don't seem happy about asking me this."

"I am, or I will be when you say yes."

Knowing there was more to this than he was letting on, she persisted, eyes roaming his face, feverishly attempting to see inside him. "If there's any element of honor or duty or anything else involved here—"

"All my honor and duty and everything else I am *are* all about you." She started to protest and his lips silenced hers, before he pulled back to pledge, "You're everything to me, Anastasia, everything. I love you. I have always and will always love you. Only ever you."

"Oh, God, Ivan, I love you, too. You're everything to me, too. You have always been and will always be. But—"

"No buts, *moya lyubov*, my love."

"Yes, Ivan, but. These things you never told me are still like a rock on your chest, a constant crushing pain. I *feel* them and they hurt me, too. They're *not* in your past, but very much in your present and I love you too much to let you carry them into your future. I want you with every fiber of my being and I was coming to tell you I'd do anything to be with you. But I won't let you spare me, I won't let you hide your pain and suffering from me anymore."

Ivan knew this was it. She wouldn't be satisfied with any more evasions. She couldn't bear any more uncertainty, wouldn't let him carry the burden alone any longer.

Feeling he'd be tearing out thorns that had been long embedded deep in his flesh, where scar tissue had formed layers that now had to be ripped open to extract them, he stalled.

"Say yes first, Anastasia. Say you'll marry me."

"This isn't about me now, Ivan. This is about you. Let me in all the way, my love, let me heal you like you healed me."

At his butchered groan, she contained him in such tenderness, such magnanimity that he'd never known existed, or that he'd ever be blessed enough to experience.

Kissing his brow, the voice he now lived to hear shook with all of her love and allegiance. "Be with me completely, Ivan. Be mine like I'm yours, past, present and future."

Capitulating once and for all, he surrendered all that he was.

His secrets, his sins, his suffering.

Down to the last mutilating detail.

Nine

Anastasia thought she'd known the worst kind of devastation when Alex had been murdered.

But there seemed to be more kinds that were just as horrifying. And even more shocking.

Ivan. His past. What had been done to him. What he'd had to endure. What he'd been made to do. What he'd had to do to escape, to rebuild himself, to build his life and power.

If she'd tried to guess for as long as she lived, she would have never imagined anything of this nature or magnitude.

But what was too terrible for her to contemplate was not what had been done to him. But by whom. His parents. The parents he'd loved and idolized. The people she'd known all her life, who'd been as much a part of her being as her own parents, and whom she'd loved and trusted almost as much.

And it explained everything. Everything. About him, who he was, how he'd come to be this way, what he could do. It explained his actions, past and present. Why he'd left her, why he'd stayed away even though he'd needed her and Alex in his life, why he'd tortured himself with depriving himself of them. Because he couldn't bear to be near the people who'd bought their own lives at the price of his.

And it explained his turmoil now. If anything was a testament to his love, it was that he'd come offering his heart, his life. He would endure the torture of living that life close to the family that had betrayed and abandoned him in this unspeakable way, just to be with her.

Now the tears that had seeped out of her soul as she'd listened to him, as she'd tried to process the enormity of his injuries, stopped, as she was hit with another realization. Ivan didn't want vengeance. He'd never wished to punish the people he'd trusted most and who'd sent him to hell.

But *she* did.

She wanted to tear down the whole world to avenge him. Since she couldn't, she'd tear down her own world.

She wiped at her tears angrily, but when she rose from her slump in Ivan's arms and looked down at him, what she saw in his eyes almost caused her heart to burst with outrage. That look of vulnerability, of defeat. She suspected what it signified.

He validated her suspicion. "I've been running away all these years from my dread of this look in your eyes, this revulsion when you realized what I really am, what I've done."

Before she could shout a vehement correction, he rose from the bed where he'd poured out his heart and horrors, turned away as if he could no longer meet her eyes.

"But you were right in persisting to make me tell you the truth. You had a right to know what kind of man I am, where I'm coming from. It would have been unfair to you if I let you marry me without knowing what you'd be really getting. I love you too much I feared it would alienate you, if not at once then later. But it's no excuse—"

She grabbed him, spastic hands sinking in the rock-hard flesh of his arms as she snatched him around to face her. "Stop, Ivan, *stop*. It's all for *you*, for the horrors you've endured, for the childhood you've lost. This is sympathy that my heart and my whole being aren't big enough to hold. But the revulsion you see? It's all for those who've done this to you."

The hesitant hope in his eyes, something she'd never thought to see tainting his indomitable wolf-like gaze, made her want to smash everything in sight.

"I love you, Ivan!" This was almost a scream. "I've loved you since I first laid eyes on you, loved you all through the years when I thought you'd abandoned me, and loved you way more when you came back and snatched me from death's jaws, then dragged me back to life. But now that I know everything, now that

I understand what drove you, what you are, I love you far more than ever before. *So* much more than I thought I could withstand. But it kills me to imagine what you've been through. It's driving me crazy to know I'd never be able to do anything about it, that I can't reach back in time and rescue the child you were. I hate it, violently, insanely, that I'm helpless to heal the man you are."

His face crumpled in such agonizing relief it made her burst into tears again. The need to protect him from even one more single moment of pain overwhelmed her, made her charge him, pushing him down again on the bed, raining her agony and reiterating her I-love-yous and I'm-sorrys on him.

His powerful arms trembled around her as if he couldn't believe she was still really there, and really feeling this way. And her rage spiked again.

She tore away from his kisses, seethed, "I might not be able to do anything about your past, but I can and will do something from now on. This crime your parents committed against you was macabre, unforgivable. And though no punishment could ever be enough, I will do everything in my power to see them punished."

He surged to cup her face, the eyes she adored urgent, anxious. "*Nyet, moya dusha*, no! I never wanted to punish them."

"Because you're far better and stronger than I am. They have to be punished, Ivan. They can't get away with this!"

"It doesn't matter anymore. And you're wrong. You

have healed me. Just seeing you like this, knowing you still love me and aren't horrified by my past, everything that's ever happened to me has ceased to exist. The one thing that burdened me was my fear of scaring you off if you found out. Of losing you. But now that I know it not only didn't matter to you, but you feel this powerfully about it all, about me, nothing else matters." He kissed her trembling tear-wet lips when she started to protest again. "As for my parents...I never wanted to see them, thought I couldn't be around them. But now that you know, now that I know you'll be mine no matter what, I don't mind having them around."

"*I* mind. Even if you've forgiven and forgotten, I can't risk that you'd feel even a twinge of heartache around them, not for the world. And *I* can't be around them either. If I'm around my parents, around Cathy and the kids, they'll *always* be around." She rose on her knees, grabbed his hands in a convulsive grip when he started to protest. "Marry me, Ivan, today, right now, and let's go back to Russia. Or anywhere in the world you want."

Then her streaking thoughts shrieked to a halt. "God, Ivan, I just realized something even more terrible. The people who sacrificed their own firstborn shouldn't be around Alex's children! They should be exposed to my family for the monsters they are so they'd be cast out of everyone's lives."

"Anastasia, please, just let it go. You can't believe Alex's children are in any danger of them. They've been exemplary parents to my siblings, and doting grandparents."

"They've been my and Alex's second parents!" she wailed. "If you could only see how they loved Alex, how they treated him like a beloved son...after they'd thrown *you* away to certain death or worse. Oh, God!"

He pressed her to his heart again, stroking her back, her hair, crooning words of comfort. After everything he'd endured, *he* was trying to soothe *her*.

"I've always understood what drove them to sacrifice me," he said, his voice now more than calm. Peaceful. "It *was* a deadly situation, and they had to make a terrible choice. I never had any wish to confront or expose them and now more than ever I see absolutely no reason to. I'm the one who caused you and I all the heartache, not them, when I let my hangups and fears of my past deprive me of you, deprive us of each other. And I'm never doing that again. I also don't want you to give up anything for me. I want you to have your family and friends and everything that makes your life normal and whole. I only wish to share it with you."

Her still-mushrooming outrage choked her all over again. "There is no going back to normal for me, not after I learned the truth about what happened to you!"

He caught her trembling face in a cherishing grip. "I only told you so you'd have access to every corner of me, so there would be no part of me you didn't see, didn't own. Not so you can wallow in a past I already intended to leave behind. My love for you fills me, heals me, makes me whole in ways I could have never dreamed I'd be. And I want us to never look back, to move only forward." His lips clung to hers, as if he needed the contact to breathe. "All you have to do now is tell me everything you wish for in a wedding and in a home for us and I'll make it happen. Even if you want it today, right now, I'll make it all happen."

"You know I want only you."

"See this?" He made a sweeping gesture at her, them, his smile exquisite. "What you feel? This is reward and cure enough to erase ten times the injuries and injustices I've suffered. But you will be my bride, and we will have a wedding, and you will have your family with you. After their incalculable loss of Alex, we can't let them lose you, too. They deserve to be happy for you."

And for the next hour she argued, cried and bargained, unable to think how she'd let him out of this room, how she'd expose him to his parents, who she knew were coming to dinner.

But he patiently, persistently, adoringly countered her every protest on his behalf.

Then at long last, she realized.

This was part of *his* healing.

This was how he'd truly move on.

"Getting married? Next week?"

Those were the exclamations that met Anastasia's announcement at the dinner table.

She didn't know which stunned her and Ivan's parents more. That they were getting married at all, or that they'd set their wedding date for six days from now, which also happened to be Christmas.

He'd finally convinced her not to elope, to have a

wedding where all the people in her life would take part. She'd succumbed only because she knew this was important to him and she wanted to give him whatever he wished for. Once that was decided on, he'd messaged his brothers. Six days from today was the earliest he could round them all up.

She looked at Ivan now, her eyes asking if he'd like to say something, but he only gave a slight nod, giving her full control over the situation.

She swept a glance around the table, her gaze unable to rest on Ivan's parents. She now hated them, and hated how Ivan must be feeling sitting so close to them. It amazed her all over again that he didn't show any emotion that even she could detect, nothing in his eyes and vibe but adoration for her.

To honor his wish to make this as normal and smooth as possible, she forced herself to flash a smile at her parents. "I hope that was you being surprised in a good way."

"God, darling, yes!" Her mother's stunned eyes shone with tears as she reached out to squeeze her hand, before turning to her father. "We're thrilled. Aren't we, dear?"

Her father nodded dazedly. "It's just that we didn't know what was going on. And it's so soon we won't have time to do much."

She waved her father's concern away. "There isn't much to do."

She had to make that perfectly clear upfront. Her parents had always dreamed of giving her as elaborate a wedding as Alex's, but with her seeming to be a bachelorette for life, she'd long thwarted them. If she gave them half a chance, they'd go all out. Ivan, too, would go to lengths she couldn't even conceive of to give her a legendary ceremony if she let him.

"We're going to keep it very simple." Before her parents or Ivan could voice any objections, she added, "I actually didn't want a wedding at all."

Because of Alex went unspoken but heard by all.

"When Ivan proposed a few hours ago I suggested we just inform you over dinner and elope." At everyone's gasps, she reached for Ivan's hand. "So you've got Ivan to thank that we'll have a wedding. He insisted that Alex wouldn't have wanted us to get married without one. But even had everything been perfect, I'm not one for frills, as you all know. I just want a gathering where everyone we love would be present."

She had to stop to swallow the bitterness that would now perpetually fill her throat. They'd both have to bear his parents' presence at their wedding, smile and pretend that everything was okay.

"Thank you, Ivan." That was her mother, turning to Ivan, her gaze filled with so much Anastasia couldn't fathom. Though she could guess. This was the man who'd saved her daughter, would now marry her and become a new son, after she'd lost her own. It must be all emotionally tumultuous for her. "I doubt any of us would have been able to change Ana's mind."

Ivan gave such a gracious smile. "It's my pleasure and privilege, Mrs. Shepherd. Quite literally."

"Please, call me Grace." Her mother gave Ivan a

wary, wavering smile. "And thank you for giving us the chance to see Ana becoming a bride."

Fixing her with a warm gaze, he covered the hand she had placed on the table. "Every mother and father should be there when a man offers his heart and life to their daughter."

A murmur of appreciation went around the table as another wave of searing love filled Anastasia's heart.

She was on the verge of tears, when Ivan's father, who'd been her beloved Uncle John until a few hours ago, rose to his feet, his face splitting on a delighted smile. "We need to toast the bride and groom!"

Ivan's mother, Aunt Glenda to her, and until so recently almost as close to Anastasia as her own mother, followed her husband, enthusiastically sweeping around the table and filling everyone's glasses with the sparkling white wine her father had selected to go with the seafood.

As she filled Ivan's glass, she squeezed his shoulder, looking down at him in such awe and affection. "You're going to be as good as my son-in-law, too, do you know that?"

Anastasia winced at the sight Ivan made with the woman who'd abandoned him, the skewer in her heart turning as she realized their green eyes were almost the same.

She battled to keep tears at bay as he looked up at his mother. Then he made it almost impossible when his face shockingly gentled as he patted her hand, the same unexpected and agonizing kindness in his voice.

"Anyone who loves Anastasia can count on me as the best relative they can have."

Looking delighted, his mother beamed down at him. "And as the one Anastasia loves most you're going to be deluged in new relatives yourself. Good thing you can't have enough family!"

Fiery indignation on his behalf lashed her, flinging the sharp words out of her mouth. "Ivan doesn't have *any* family."

Ivan raised his glass to her, his gaze soothing her. "The only important thing to me is that I'll now have one with you, my love." He looked around the room, his gaze containing nothing but genuine geniality. "And clearly many extensions, too."

She nodded tightly, letting him pull her back from the brink, gratitude engulfing her that he was giving her the opportunity to make it all up to him for the rest of her life.

But as if to further inflame her, his mother touched his shoulder again, her eyes probing, pained. "Are you an orphan?"

There was no use. She couldn't hold back. And she didn't.

"Worse. His parents abandoned him."

His parents had the gall to look horrified.

Then Aunt Glenda whispered, "That's *terrible.* Were you very young? What happened to you?"

Clearly deciding to put an end to this, Ivan rose and turned to his parents with an easy smile Anastasia had no idea how he managed. "As you can see

I far more than survived. Now I found the biggest part of my soul and I am the happiest man on earth."

Uncle John, his father, looking as if he'd dodged a bullet, laughed and raised his glass. "And now you do have more family than you'll know what to do with. You have two fathers-in-law and two mothers-in-law and a bunch of in-laws—siblings, nieces and nephews. Before this alarms you, let me assure you it's a bargain. We're full of uses, all ready and eager to do any amount of chores and babysit on demand. And we're only slightly interfering."

Her father rose with a wide smile, raising his own glass. "Ivan doesn't strike me as the kind of son-in-law who'd allow *any* level of interference."

Ivan returned her father's smile. "Not even from a superpower."

Swallowing down her agitation, Anastasia volunteered the explanation. "He's not being metaphorical here. Remind me to tell you about the time when he blithely ignored the Russian premier's demand for a personal meeting because he thought babysitting *me* was more important."

All voices rose around the table, demanding she tell the story immediately. And in telling it, she and Ivan relaxed back into their flawless rapport, and what she never thought could happen did. The night turned into an immensely enjoyable interlude, especially when Cathy and the kids came over.

For long stretches of time during the night that extended into the early hours of morning, Anastasia found herself forgetting everything but that she was with the people she loved most on earth, the people who surrounded the union she was forging with Ivan with delight and caring.

But every now and then, the illusion cracked and she saw the truth. The truth that was uglier than anything from a nightmare. Ivan bolstered her, absorbing her agitation as soon as it surged. But even if he'd dealt so incredibly well with what he'd lived dreading—seeing his parents up-close again—she could not do the same.

After their wedding, she would never expose him to them again if she could at all help it. His parents didn't deserve the happiness and privilege of knowing him as he'd made himself, didn't deserve his unbelievable mercy.

With the countdown to the wedding rushing by, Anastasia found herself sliding into stretches of absolute euphoria.

Being with Ivan now that she was certain of his love was a happiness she hadn't known could exist.

He, too, seemed on a constant high.

Yet, it still came in waves. That tension, like a sick buzz of electricity that zapped her muscles, a white noise that scratched along her nerves. Ivan kept assuring her it wasn't coming from him, that he was fine, that being with her had nullified anything he'd feared he'd feel. He not only didn't feel anything negative around his parents, as strange as it might sound, he actually enjoyed being with them.

And then they'd found there was a bonus that neither of them had considered. His siblings.

Cathy and the others, with all their kids, were all over him, as if they recognized he was kindred. This complicated Anastasia's original plan of moving away as soon as the ceremony was over and seeing their families as little as possible. Ivan deserved to have the pleasure of knowing his siblings and being part of their lives, to bask in their eagerness and admiration, in what she knew would turn to love.

And today of all days, it did feel as if it would be impossible to just walk away from their families.

Debating how to handle or time making this disclosure, she walked into the great room that overlooked the Atlantic and found Ivan looking out to the horizon, in one of the rare times she'd found him alone since they'd come here.

Ivan had invited everyone to stay in his Hamptons estate, where they'd have the wedding. He'd been constantly waving his magic wand to give everyone an experience that would never be equaled, mixing the holiday season celebrations with what he called "wedding overtures."

When she objected that this was all a far cry from the simple couple of hours she'd expected for the wedding ceremony, he just kissed her and demanded she appreciate his "restraint", reminding her what it was like when he was extravagant.

His brothers would be arriving a day before the ceremony, and she couldn't wait to see the rest of that unique brotherhood who'd shared Ivan's tragic origins, and who had not only triumphed over unimaginable hardships, but also, like him, had gone on to conquer the world in their own fields of virtuosity.

Feeling a wave of love crash on her harder than those on the beach below, she slid her arms around him from the back. To her amazement, he was surprised. Ivan had always been primed, feeling the slightest movement from afar, even before it happened. He'd certainly never been oblivious to her approach, seemed to feel it when it was only an intention in her mind. That he'd been now meant he'd been too consumed by something.

Her heart started hammering with worry. But he was turning to her, plucking her up and into a kiss that, as usual, overwhelmed her.

When he finally let her feet touch the ground again, her hands roved over his rock-hard body, still uneasy. "You okay?"

"I am now." He gave her another mind-melting kiss. "There's a lot more to take in than even I thought."

She knew what he meant. His family. "Is that why you were off in another realm? Why you're so tense?"

"I was lost in thought, yes. But I'm tense because I'm not making love to you. That is making me downright dangerous. You do remember I put my libido in a deep freeze for years, and now I'm constantly burning. So this—" he brought her hands to his body, sliding them down his chest to his erection, each inch the consistency of steel "—is because of you."

She pouted. "Whose idea was it to not make love to me?"

He huffed in self-deprecation. "I *do* get stupid

ideas. Always concerning you. I thought I could last a week with all the preparations and the family and friends around to distract me. Especially since their presence isn't conducive to our kind of explosive encounters. I also thought the torment of abstinence will serve a purpose, make sure I'd give you a wedding night to remember for the next few lifetimes."

"I'll remember each night with you longer than that."

At her hotly aroused statement, he devoured her again.

He was kissing her within an inch of her sanity when her parents walked in. Groaning, they separated, even as her parents started retreating in embarrassment.

But since she did have to try on dresses, and pick one of the dozen Ivan had provided her, she decided to postpone what she'd sought him for, said she was the one who had to go. Her parents accompanied her.

As they walked out, she again felt her parents' subdued melancholy and lingering unease.

Like her, they hadn't truly gotten over Alex's death. And though she had reassured them she knew what she was doing, marrying a man whose rivals called him Ivan the Terrible, who had enough power to tackle a world leader, it was evident they were still worried. She also suspected that even though she'd expanded on the story he'd provided about her and Alex's accident, they still felt something was off about it and about his role in the whole thing.

But since the truth would only hurt them more, she couldn't allay their suspicions. Not now, not ever.

A couple of hours later, after she'd drowned in fairy-tale gowns and picked the one that made her feel least guilty to wear only months after she'd lost Alex, everyone gathered for another of Ivan's exquisitely catered dinners.

Much later, after the younger generation and their kids went to bed, only she, Ivan and their parents remained.

Ivan took the men to the pool table, and she found herself alone with her mother and his.

As each sat sipping her choice of herbal tea, his mother turned from watching the men and looked back at Anastasia.

"You know, Ana, ever since I first saw Ivan there's been this…overwhelming feeling that comes over me whenever I look at him. And it's not because he's the most powerful and important man I'll ever meet in my life. There's just something about him."

Gritting her teeth, Anastasia said, "Yeah, it's called charisma and influence. He makes everyone feel this way."

Aunt Glenda sat up closer, her eyes so earnest. "It's not that, though I do recognize this about him. There's just this…huge side to him I feel he's hiding."

"Yes, exactly." That was Anastasia's mother, sitting up on her other side, making her feel they were squeezing her in the middle with their curiosity and concern. "It's like there's another person beneath it all.

Are you aware of that? Do you know who he really is under this…facade?"

"It's not like I'm worried that he doesn't love you as completely as you love him—" Aunt Glenda stopped, seemed to be getting more distressed the more she tried to explain. "It's just… I wonder about what he's hiding. I know it's crazy, but what I feel…" She looked back at him and fell silent.

So recognition *was* haunting her, despite the transfiguring changes he'd undergone, through ordeals, maturation and intention. And she was disturbed, groping for explanations, something to make her feel secure again in the safe, suburban life she'd built, and paid for with his life.

Aunt Glenda looked back at her, putting down her cup, looking frustrated, even agitated. "God, I wish I could explain it. I wish I knew what I was feeling."

Every word had been falling on Anastasia like a scythe, slashing every fiber of restraint.

The last words severed the final tether, and she snapped.

Heaving up to her feet, she shouted, "What you're feeling is recognition, Aunt Glenda. Recognition of the son you sold to slavers, in return for a way out of Russia and a new life in the States. Slavers who tortured, degraded and exploited him in unimaginable ways!"

Ivan had picked up the feeling that something was going wrong across the room. He'd excused himself from his companions at once and had started rushing there even before he realized what was going on.

But it all happened before he could stop it. Anastasia was on her feet, screaming, everything—*everything*—pouring out of her.

He was running now, feeling both their fathers in his wake, cold sweat starting to bead on his forehead, knowing that whatever he did now, it was too late.

Anastasia sounded as if she was tearing apart her vocal chords. "How dare you sit there pretending you're a normal person? A woman and a mother? A human being even? That you have any kind of feelings? You sold your son! Your firstborn! The genius boy who loved you completely and trusted you implicitly!"

Ivan finally reached Anastasia, put himself between her and the others, taking her by the shoulders, tried to make her look at him, to silence her. "Stop. Anastasia, stop. Come with me, please."

But she only pushed against him, twisting in his hold, around his bulk, seeking to reconnect her wrath with its targets, eyes feverish between both his parents now, shaking so hard it was like she was having a seizure. Her voice had become a butchered wail, again making him realize what she now knew of his past hurt her even more than it had ever hurt him.

"Didn't you ever think of the devastation he felt when he realized you betrayed and bartered him? Didn't you ever feel sorry all these years that you sent your own son to hell, to buy yourselves this easy, petty life? Didn't you ever imagine the kind of horrors he faced, the agony and desperation he endured?" She lurched out of his hold completely, no longer

Anastasia, but a rage-filled entity as she shrieked her condemnations. "And after everything you did to him—after he overcame it all and became the best man on earth—he never wanted revenge, only never wanted to see you again. *That's* why he lost seven more years of his life, when he could have been with me. He only found me again through tragedy. And for me, he not only let himself be exposed to you, he did what I thought impossible. He was kind to you. He *forgave* you. When you're *monsters*! Monsters who don't even deserve to live!"

Ivan had dragged her in his arms as she screamed, but had been unable to stop her tirade. He now subdued her efforts to fight him away, pressing her head into his chest, murmuring pleas for her to stop. He had to stem the tide of wrath and misery that was undoing her right before his eyes.

But she'd already expended every last spark of energy, now sagged against him, too drained to even tremble anymore.

It was only after he made sure this paroxysm was over, and he'd carried her to the nearest couch, soothed and revived her as much as he could, that he finally remembered the presence of the others.

Turning his gaze, he found them all frozen in their exact positions. His parents looked as if their hearts had been ripped out, their faces blank in that shocked denial before the injury registered and the collapse occurred.

"K-Konstantin? Kostya?"

His mother sounded as if someone was choking

her as she said his name, and the nickname she'd used to call him with.

Giving Anastasia one last kiss, begging her again not to move, to let him handle this, he rose to his feet.

There was no escaping it anymore. Here was the confrontation he'd lived almost three decades dreading.

Coming to stand before his parents, he nodded. "It's me."

Looking as if they thought they were losing their minds, they reached out their hands to him, as if to make sure he was real.

"That's—that's the explanation for wh-what our hearts have been telling us about you…"

"We thought you were lost to us all these years ago…"

His beyond shell-shocked parents talked over each other, then stopped.

Then his father's face crumpled as he staggered back as if under a bone-crushing blow. He would have fallen on the ground if Ivan hadn't caught him and lowered him onto an armchair.

The moment he straightened, his mother was clawing at him, crying, then bawling such ugly, violent sobs he felt as if she was being torn apart inside.

Ivan had dealt with death, with danger and violence of the most extreme magnitudes. But against tears, especially Anastasia's and now his mother's, he was totally powerless.

Looking around, as if seeking help, he found Anastasia staring at him limply. Her parents had sat down, looked as if they'd turned to stone. No help was coming from any of them.

Forcing himself to contain his mother, he led her to sit in the armchair next to his father, who was weeping, too, silent tears that were somehow even more distressing to Ivan.

Knowing this had to end, once and for all, he went down on his haunches before them. "My view of this isn't as harsh as Anastasia. She's angry on my behalf, far more than I've ever been on my own. I understood you made a terrible decision, to save Katerina and Fedora and Ivanna and Dimitri, not only yourselves. And maybe you didn't realize what would happen, what they'd do to me. But as I told you before, I survived, and then some. And now I have Anastasia, and I love her and I am happy with her, beyond comprehension. I know it won't be easy, living with this now that the past is exhumed, but—"

His father lurched forward, his hand trembling to Ivan's face, his eyes blood-red. "We believed that you died."

Ivan's jaw clenched. "It was always a possibility to die there."

His father shook his head vigorously. "No, no, we were told you died in a car accident before you even reached the academy you were supposed to join, what we fully believed was a legitimate institution."

Ivan stared at him. Did he mean…?

"We never suspected *anything* of what Ana said. We thought we lost you to a senseless accident like we lost Alex!"

His mother again snatched at anything she could hold of him, ended up grabbing his jacket, his shirt, his hair. "You thought we abandoned you? Sold you? *Bozhe moy…*"

She burst into another jag of demolishing weeping as she pitched forward to kiss his hand and bathe it in her tears.

As he tried to drag his hand away, his heart stuttering in his chest, his father grabbed his other hand.

"It was years before we could get over our grief and guilt for sending you somewhere without us. Just that we weren't there for you, that we thought you died alone, almost drove us both mad. It was only having to care for our other children that forced us to continue to function. If we'd known anything about the true nature of that place, if we even suspected for a second you wouldn't get the best treatment, wouldn't be achieved and happy there, that we wouldn't see you again soon, we would have rather died than send you there."

Ivan stared at the parents he'd once loved with everything in him, whom he'd missed and felt their loss like that of a vital organ.

And he knew one thing.

They were telling the truth.

Ten

Ivan had felt his whole belief system being rewritten once before. When everything told him that his parents had abandoned him in the worst way possible.

Now everything said they hadn't. Every cell in his body screamed it, had been screaming it since he'd looked into their eyes again.

The knowledge was absolute, incontrovertible.

This time no amount of circumstantial evidence would convince him differently.

And it was like an earthquake was unleashed inside him, sending everything crashing, the pillars he'd built his life around collapsing, pulverizing each other and everything else.

He vaguely realized the pain he was feeling was only the beginning of a process that would reform his memories, his psyche. There was no escaping letting the process take its course, no ameliorating the pangs of this excruciating rebirth.

He could only do one thing.

Kneeling before his parents, his hands shook as he took a hand from each, his heart squeezing as he felt how fragile they'd become. This wasn't only a sign of aging, it was the unremitting effects of loss.

His loss. He knew it.

He let them know he did. "I believe you. And I will never be able to beg your forgiveness enough for believing any differently of you. My only excuse is that it was horrific, not only being in that hellhole, but being without you. I guess at first I needed to believe you sacrificed me so I could let you go, and let hope and life itself go, so I'd escape my prison. Later I needed to believe it so it would harden me, so I could survive."

His parents collapsed over him, deluging him in the agony of their tears, disbelief, relief…and love.

Feeling as helpless as he had when he'd arrived too late to save Alex, unable to rewind the past and erase the damage, he hugged them with all he was.

"Forgive me for suspecting you, for depriving us of all these years we could have been together since my escape."

They both wept and shook and hugged him back until he felt their long-fractured hearts splintering again. He had to stop the vicious circle of pain and regret, had to start them on the path of healing.

Pulling back, he forced a smile on his numb lips.

"But I know you'll forgive me, even if I don't deserve to be forgiven. I know because I'm blessed like that. I committed the same crime with Anastasia. I deprived her of seven years when I could have loved and worshipped her, because of my hang-ups and misjudgments. And she not only forgave me, she saved me and promised to love me forever."

He looked back at her, found her sitting up rigidly, her face gripped in a storm of emotions. Dominating all was love. For him. And for his parents. And such relief. But it was the total lack of recrimination, the absolute alliance and understanding that she gave him unconditionally that gave him the ability to forgive himself, so he could give his all to her, to his parents.

Knowing she wouldn't intrude on these moments with his parents without an invitation, he reached out an arm to her, begging her nearness, letting her know there was no breath he wanted to take without her.

She staggered up to her feet and hurtled toward him unsteadily, throwing herself at him. It was like catching life itself when he wrapped her in his arms. She was more than that to him. She was the reason for, and the orchestrator of, his rebirth.

Then she was reaching out to include his parents in their embrace. Her apologies were as pained and profuse as much as their dismissal and their thanks. They insisted it was because she loved Ivan so much that she couldn't bear thinking he'd go unavenged that this all had come to light, and been resolved.

Surrounding them all in his protection and love, Ivan looked at his parents. "I need you to put it all behind us, to only look forward. Anastasia taught me this, too."

His mother burst into another jag of sobs. "I can *never* forget or live with what happened to you."

He pulled her tighter into his embrace, soothing her renewed anguish. "Whatever I went through, it all worked out for the absolute best. And it's not because I became so much stronger or because I'm now wealthy and powerful, it's because of this." He gave the most precious people in his life, the reasons for it, another squeeze, making them all shudder in relief. "Finding Anastasia, loving her, having her love, and reuniting with both of you—these miracles far surpass my ordeals, erases them. I even think it's only fair to have paid that price in advance, for your priceless blessing. So just love me like I love you, and let me make you all happy again."

For an interminable time afterward, Anastasia and Ivan's parents flooded him in every poignant and thankful emotion and he submerged them in the endlessness of his love.

Then, feeling it was the beginning of a new life for real, she knew it was the right time to take it up that final notch.

Rising from the couch where he'd taken them, where she'd been plastered to him with his parents on his other side, she stood before him.

"All this?" She gestured between them and to his parents and around the room to hers. "It only gets better. You have one more miracle coming."

Vulnerability flooded his face once again, as if he was still afraid, would always be unable to believe he could possibly have all this. She had a feeling he understood what she was about to tell him. And could barely bear the enormity of even contemplating it.

Drowning into his emerald eyes, she pulled him up and shared what she'd discovered right before she'd gone searching for him this afternoon. "Yes, *moy lyubov*, you'll have one more person to love and who will love you forever. I'm pregnant."

The extent of Ivan's jubilation at her news continued to stun Anastasia.

Two nights ago when she'd announced her pregnancy, he'd looked as if he was disintegrating under the brunt of too much joy. After promising his parents that they'd continue talking later when he wasn't literally out of his mind with exultation, he'd swept her to his bed.

Not that he'd made love to her. They'd both been too hectic with emotions they'd just needed to be wrapped in each other's arms, to attempt to contain it all and come back down to earth.

He'd made love to her the next morning, though, taking them both to the very edge of their mortality. He'd said he was done waiting for their wedding night, even if it was only one more day away. He claimed that if he'd waited, she wouldn't have had a groom to walk down the aisle to. Not a correctly functioning one, at least. And she'd wholeheartedly approved his strategy.

Now there were less than twenty-four hours to Christmas day, and their wedding.

Dragging themselves from the depths of satiation she and Ivan had just reluctantly left his suite. According to the many messages he'd gotten throughout the night, all his brothers had arrived. According to the many knocks on the door they'd had, everyone gathered downstairs was waiting for them to have an early Christmas since their wedding had confiscated the actual date.

They now descended along one arm of the bifurcated marble stairs, to an incredible sight.

That of everyone they both loved.

And they all did something that made her burst into tears again.

They treated her and Ivan to a standing ovation.

Feeling her knees buckling, she clung harder to Ivan. He swept her up in his arms at once, as if he'd been itching for an excuse to do so, drowned her in a kiss that sent the whole world spinning.

She clung around his neck and kissed him back as deeply to the background music of raucous cheers and hoots. She vaguely discerned the unfamiliar voices among those of her family and friends. Those of his brothers and their wives.

Curiosity and impatience to see those men who'd shared so much with Ivan, who were a major reason he'd survived, had become the incomparable force of nature he was now, overwhelmed her. It would have taken nothing less to make her cut their kiss short.

Looking avidly at the crowd as Ivan resumed descending the stairs with her still high up in his arms, she almost gasped. The collective of his brothers, now on their feet, was staggering. It was as if she was looking at different versions of Ivan.

She was thrilled to see Dr. Balducci—Tonio as Ivan called him and insisted she did, too. Now his terrible misunderstanding with Liliana had been resolved, and she was now his wife, he looked on top of the world. The others she recognized at once from Ivan's descriptions of them. Each was totally unique. Yet they all looked as if they'd been made from the same higher-being material. As they had. They'd all been chosen by The Organization for being prodigies, then they'd been forged in the inferno of ordeals into the best and most powerful versions of themselves.

And those men had in turn picked women who were clearly their perfect match. Each woman stood beside her man, as magnificent as he was in her own way. She only hoped she looked anywhere near as worthy and fitting standing next to Ivan.

Everyone let the newcomers approach Ivan and her first. Ivan put her down on her feet so she could meet them. Not knowing how to welcome those formidable beings who towered over everyone, she started with Antonio Balducci, extending her hand, lips splitting in delight at seeing him again. And he set the rules for this encounter. Her former surgeon and savior pulled her into an affectionate hug, telling her that he'd be her brother-in-law now. His new bride, Liliana, followed suit, expressing her delight that she'd have yet another sister.

The rest of the introductions were as enthusiastic and warmhearted, with her being hugged and kissed and doted on by all, even his brothers' children. There was quite the array of them. Raiden and Scarlett had six alone, adopted and biological. The others had two or three and a couple were working on the next one. Even the newest wife, Liliana, was clearly pregnant. And when Anastasia expressed how incredible it was her and Ivan's baby would be born to find so many brothers and sisters, she was exposed to another round of deluging delight and indulgence.

After they judged Ivan's brothers and their families had gotten enough exclusive time with her and Ivan, the rest converged on them. Or really mostly on Ivan. His sisters and brother and their spouses and children more or less carried him off like they'd been doing the past few days whenever they could, unable to get enough of him. And that when they had no idea who he really was to them.

No one but both their parents knew, or would know of last night's revelations, at least until they all agreed on how to break out the news that Ivan was family in more ways that they thought.

After what she could only describe as the best Christmas lunch in the history of the planet, everyone decided it was time to open presents.

And there were *so* many presents. Everyone had bought presents for everyone else. His brothers and their wives had done their homework to such a meticulous level, no doubt with Ivan's insider's help, they'd gotten every single one of her extended family a unique, incredibly suitable, not to mention lavish gift.

Then came her own present. Something she couldn't have even imagined.

The brotherhood were offering her The Alex Shepherd Research Division, a whole new arm of Black Castle Enterprises that she'd build and helm to Alex's specs and in his memory.

It took hours for her, and for her family, to really wrap their mind around the enormity of this gift.

At one point when she'd barely recovered her wits, she realized one strange thing. Apart from her own gift from the brotherhood—which she was certain had been orchestrated by Ivan—he was the only one who'd gotten no one anything.

Which didn't make sense whatsoever with him being such an extravagant giver.

Which meant one thing. He was keeping his own gifts to everyone for last.

As she wondered what they would be, and when he'd present them, he stood up and invited everyone to dress warmly and follow him into the garden overlooking the ocean.

As everyone rushed after him, it only took stepping outside for everyone to freeze to the spot and gape at the sight before them.

The garden, now covered in snow, had been turned into a Christmas wonderland.

Ivan rushed down the stairs with her dazed beside him, encouraging everyone to follow suit. As soon as everyone descended into the garden, two musical bands, each made of two-dozen musicians and as many singers started playing Christmas carols and songs. The whole place had been turned into an amusement park complete with carousels and rides for both children and adults. And interspersing everything, dozens of *gigantic* Christmas trees towered, magically decorated and lit. Beneath each tree, there were *huge* heaps of gift boxes in the most exquisite wrappings she'd ever seen.

She had no idea when he'd had all his done. Just last night none of that was there. Hell, it wasn't there two hours ago when she'd last caught a glimpse of the garden.

Everyone, even his brothers, seemed to be transported into the fairytale ambiance Ivan had so meticulously created. Shrieks of delight echoed from the children, and laughter from the adults.

Dazed at yet another staggering display of his resources and thoughtfulness, she looked up at him as everyone rushed here and there to sample his wonderland's enchantments.

"Tell me most of these boxes are part of the decorations."

He bent and covered her now-cold lips in his warm ones, singeing her blood and making her forget a world outside him existed as always.

Letting her lips go with one last clinging kiss, he withdrew, teased, "You know I'll do anything you want. You want me to lie, I will."

She shook her head, looking around at the trees. "Even if you got every single person multiple Christmas presents, it still wouldn't explain those…mountains!"

He swept her off her feet again and headed for one of the carousels where all his brothers were taking their children for a ride.

"I did get everyone more than one present. Including everyone who works here and their families, all the event-planning people preparing our wedding tomorrow, the catering team and the music bands and anyone who had a hand in all this."

She jumped up in his arms and drowned him in kisses and love and thanks, on behalf of everyone he'd thought of.

Laughing, he stepped on the revolving carousel's platform and raised her on top of one of the undulating horses. Effortlessly jumping up behind her, he wrapped his arms around her, his hands caressing her were the evidence of their love was growing into a new life.

Putting his lips to her ears so she'd hear him over the lively holiday music and singing and the myriad sounds of joy, he said, "How about you make the rounds telling everyone you've already thanked me on their behalf? Now that I think about it, the number of projected thank yous is making me reconsider giving anyone anything."

She threw her head back on his shoulder, looked up at him, saw the edge of real aversion and anxiety in his lightheartedness and grinned. "No can do."

His body tensed around her as he scowled. "If you won't save me, I'll just courier everyone their stuff."

She burrowed back deeper into his body, savoring his heat and hardness even through their thermal clothing. "No, you won't. I'll make the rounds with you as you give everyone their presents, and you'll take the gratitude you deserve like a champ." Before he could protest, she invoked that carte blanche he kept renewing every single day. "I so want to meet everyone who run this impeccable place, who made all the fabulousness of today come to life, who'll make the undisputable perfection of tomorrow. In short, all those amazing beings who actually live up to your expectations and demands."

His eyes took that intensely adoring cast she'd gotten addicted to and couldn't live without. "Anything that pleases you." Then he mock-shuddered. "Now I must take my anti-thanks medication in preparation."

She hooted with laughter. "I'll have a talk with Tonio and Liliana about developing you a vaccine."

He joined her in laughter, before they both turned to shout and laugh with his brothers and their families. Afterward, they sampled each ride, talked and laughed and played and sang with all their guests, then proceeded to distribute his tons of presents.

And all through, Ivan kept her at his side as if she was as vital to him as his beating heart. As she knew she was. As he was to her. This indescribably incredible, magnanimous man who had unbelievably chosen her to love for the rest of his life.

At the end of the enchanted day, what everyone said qualified as one of the best days of their lives, excitement and happiness were coursing through Anastasia, making her downright giddy.

But to her consternation, after all the bustle had died down, she felt as if a freezing hand was squeezing her heart.

It was that darkness that had lurked in the back of her mind, that hadn't been resolved after yesterday's revelations. That unease that had been coming to her in waves, even among the ocean of rapture of last night and today. It now surged, crested, loomed over her like a tidal wave about to crash.

She'd just entered the bedroom suite with Ivan when it did.

She had no evidence. She just *knew*. Where that dark unease had come from. And what it signified.

The truth.

What was even worse than her worst nightmares.

She had no idea how she continued interacting with Ivan until he entered the bathroom. Then feeling as if she was walking with her own two feet to the slaughter, she headed toward her parents' suite.

The moment she entered and found them both sitting there in silence, looking like automatons, the knowledge solidified.

"I felt it, Dad." Her voice sounded alien in her ears. "When the revelations were being made. Even among the upheaval, I felt it. You know something more about Ivan's past. You more than know. You had a hand in it."

Her father looked at her as if he'd sustained multiple stab wounds and was silently bleeding to death.

"It was you, wasn't it?" she rasped. "You're the one who did this. You're the one who sent Ivan to hell."

Her father rose to his feet as if from under rubble, aging before her eyes, looking as if he'd have a stroke.

"It was me."

The whispered words speared Anastasia in her gut.

Her mother.

Turning away from her father, she looked at the woman who'd given birth to her, whom she'd loved and believed in all her life.

What she saw in her mother's eyes brought her whole world crashing down, crushing her beneath its debris.

"Your father and I...we were marked for liquidation," her mother said, looking as if she'd taken a decision to end her own life. "We were beyond desperate when I learned of The Organization. I approached them for a deal, and my only bargaining chip was Kostya. He was such a prodigy... I knew they'd do anything to get their hands on him. They said if I convinced my friends to let them have him, they would get us all out of Russia and give us new lives in the States. So I made a plan to indirectly convince them that it was a great opportunity, so they would never realize it was I who initiated the bargain, or learn of its true nature or that of those I made it with.

"And there was not a single minute that passed since when I didn't regret it, not one breath that wasn't poisoned by his memory or the taste of my crime. When I thought Kostya died in that accident, I was almost relieved that fate chose to end his torment before it began. Everything I did since was aimed at trying to make it up to Glenda and John, to atone. Not that I thought anything would or could. Then I saw Ivan, and everything inside me screamed, even though it seemed impossible. I only told your father when we found out who Ivan really was."

Her mother lay down on the couch, curled up, shaking, her eyes dry. She must have already expended all her tears.

If desolation and death had a sound, they would sound like her mother did now. "I deprived my friends of their son, and fate only bided its time before finally retaliating in kind."

Then there was silence.

And in the silence, the cacophony of realizations attacked Anastasia.

Her mother had sold Ivan in return for their safety. She believed Alex had died to settle the cosmic score.

Anastasia herself had lived a life of security and freedom at the expense of Ivan's despair and degradation.

The enormity of it all held its breath over her like a vast, black cloud. Then it detonated.

And there was nothing more.

Surfacing from the nothingness was terrifying.

She wanted to remain there where she'd once hidden, where it was dark and silent, where she was sinking in an eternity of pain-free paralysis.

But oblivion was relinquishing her to awareness, expelling her to its mercilessness. She was already feeling, hearing. And once she opened her eyes, she'd see what she couldn't bear seeing. Ivan. Frantically hovering over her, going insane with worry.

From the voices with him she knew he'd brought Antonio, and Isabella, a surgeon, too, and the wife of his partner, Richard Graves. They were both assuring him she was physically perfectly fine, that fainting was not unheard of in the early months of pregnancy, especially after the physical and emotional tests she'd endured in the past months.

She pretended to be still passed out until they left, hoping Ivan would leave, too.

But she soon had to admit that he never would. The man who'd stayed by her bedside for weeks, then remained by her side since, would stay here forever. He wouldn't leave her until he made sure she was fine. When she would never be again.

Giving in, knowing that it was better to get this over with, she opened her eyes.

The look on his face translated the gnawing anxiety in his voice, making her almost close her eyes again. It hurt to see him like this, feel him caring, now that she knew the atrocious truth.

The truth that destroyed everything.

He covered her face in kisses, his tremors transmitting to her heart in shock waves of despair. "*Moya dorogoya, moya dusha*, I'm here. You're okay."

Unable to look at him anymore, she averted her gaze and nodded. "Sorry for the scare. One moment I was upright, the next everything just went dark. I'm fine now."

His fingers, gentle, persistent, caressed her cheek, tried to turn her eyes back to him. "This is my fault. I taxed you." He bit off a vicious self-imprecation. "I shouldn't have made love to you, let alone repeatedly long and hard. I'm an animal."

The shard of agony embedded in her heart twisted deeper, forcing her to look at him. She couldn't bear him feeling guilty over her, when it was on her account that her mother had consigned him to a horrific fate. She owed him a debt that could never be repaid.

"You didn't tax me, Ivan, and you know it." Before he could take her in his arms again, she rose to a sitting position so he had to pull back. "But everything *is* catching up with me and I do feel tired. I can't see myself doing much for a while. I—I think we should postpone the wedding."

Expecting him to argue, he again floored her by the extent of his consideration, agreeing at once. "Whatever you wish. If the wedding is part of what's putting stress on you, we can always gather everyone right here, exchange vows and send them on their way."

She was desperate to stop his pampering. If she didn't make a stand she'd find herself married to him within the hour.

She shook her head. "I just need a postponement. I hope nobody will be too upset."

His eyes filled with indulgence. "Everyone can cool their heels until you're feeling up to it. Don't worry about anything but feeling stronger, *moya dusha*. The world can stand still or even go away completely until then for all I care."

Feeling it would hurt less if she were the one to go away, forever, she pretended to nod and fall asleep again.

Knowing he wouldn't leave, she turned her face away from his vigilance, unable to stop the silent tears from pouring out of her soul.

It had been three days since Anastasia had fainted.

After he'd had Antonio and Isabella examine her again, and again, to reassure him she'd bounce back given time, Ivan had gathered everyone the very next morning, Christmas Day, what should have been their wedding day, and announced the postponement of their wedding.

She'd spent half that day in bed, and the other half curled in an armchair, barely saying or doing anything. The next day everyone had gone back to their homes.

Anastasia had asked to go home, too. Her parents' home. Feeling more worried and confused by the second, but wanting to give her whatever she wished for, he'd taken her there. He'd been trying to placate himself that early pregnancy, the revelations, the days among such an overwhelming crowd, had proven too strenuous for her. But every time he went to her, it became clearer, until he could no longer lie to himself.

It now pained her to see him.

But he'd been unable to ask why. He was terrified she'd tell him she was having second thoughts.

It was unimaginable, but the only reason he could think of anymore. That now she realized it was going to be real, and she'd tie herself to him for life, through marriage and through a child, his reality had finally sunk in, and she was horrified about what she'd let herself in for.

But three days in a hell of dread and uncertainty had proved his limit. Though knowing for certain would finish him, he couldn't let her evade him any longer.

He'd just arrived at her parents' home and again they weren't there. The maid had opened the door for him, telling him Anastasia had just gone up to her room.

In a matter of seconds he was knocking on her door. He'd heard her moving inside, and he had a distinctive knock, so she knew it was him. The prolonged silence that answered his knock screamed with her reluctance to let him in, to see him again.

This was it, then.

Whatever it did to him, he couldn't force himself on her. If she didn't want him anymore, if it hurt her that much to see him, he had to leave her alone.

He'd cross that threshold for the last time. When he left, he'd have no more reason to go on living.

At long last, she opened the door, and any lingering hope that he'd been wrong was incinerated under the inescapable proof of her desolation. She looked as finished as he felt.

His heart about to ram out of his rib cage with the need to take her in his arms, to beg her not to recede, not to shut him out of her heart, he met her blood-shot, swollen eyes.

"Why?" At his butchered groan, she said nothing, her breathing becoming strident. He broke down then, begged, "Is there anything I can do to make you love me again?"

She staggered back as if he'd hit her.

Surging forward to abort her stumble, he grabbed her arm, but she jerked it back as if he'd electrified her.

His arms fell limply to his side, crippled by a defeat he hadn't even felt when he'd been young and helpless and at the nonexistent mercy of the monsters who'd imprisoned him.

Breath emptied from his chest, for what felt like the last time. "I guess I was always waiting for this, for you to come to your senses."

Shaking, starting to sob, she fell to the bed. Dropping her head in her trembling hands, she rocked to and fro, moaning as if her soul was bleeding out of her.

He kneeled in front of her before he collapsed, his own soul escaping him with the tears he'd never shed since he was a child except on her account.

"Don't, Anastasia, don't do this to yourself. Don't feel sorry for me, or feel bad because you gave me hope or made me a promise. I beg you. Don't languish in bed, don't lock yourself from the world to escape your life altogether because I'm in it. I left you once when I thought I'd only bring you danger and anxiety and misery. I'll leave again, because I only want you to be happy and at peace. I just came to tell you this. That I'll always be there for you, and for our child, in any way you let me. But if it hurts you this much to see me, you don't have to see me ever again."

Her weeping escalated with her inability to draw full breaths anymore. Unable to bear her anguish, he exploded up to his feet and stumbled towards the door.

His shaking hand was on the doorknob when Anastasia's words hit him like a bullet between the shoulder blades.

"I'll tell you why. I owe you that. When you know, it will be you who won't ever want to see me again."

Anastasia watched Ivan turning around, hating her very existence even more for the destruction and defeat marring his face and slumping his body. Desecrating his soul. She'd done this to him.

Before she lost all ability to speak, she told him everything. The atrocious, crippling truth.

All through the account she tore out of the depths of her desperation and shame, he remained leaning against the wall as if he'd been riveted there, staring at her as if he couldn't understand a word she said.

By the time she reached the most relevant part, she felt she'd never stop weeping again. "I l-loved my mother until I learned of the heinous crime she'd committed against you. Now I h-hate her...want her punished. I need you to promise me you will punish her. I need you to punish *me*. I can't live knowing my life has been bought at the expense of yours."

Ivan continued to stare at her. And stare at her.

Then he finally pushed himself away from the wall, came closer with such care, as if she was holding a knife to her own throat and he was afraid she'd slit it if he moved any faster.

His voice was so hushed it was almost inaudible as he rasped, "Do you mean you still love me?"

"God, Ivan, is this the only thing you got out of everything I told you?"

"It's the only thing of any importance."

"No, God, no, you're *not* doing this. You're not brushing this aside. You're not refusing to avenge yourself again."

"You know I never wanted that. I forgave my parents even before I knew they had no hand in what happened to me."

"They're *your* parents. It's up to you to forgive them. But she's *my* mother, and you don't get to forgive her. I don't. Do you hear me? I will never forgive her. I'm leaving this house tomorrow and I'm never coming back."

He was kneeling before her again, his eyes clearing of the ravages of the tears that had made her want to inflict some serious damage on herself, his lips curving into that intimate smile that stirred her insides into mush. "Of course you're leaving this house. You'll be in *our* home, and you're coming back here only for visits."

"No, Ivan, you're *not* smiling!"

His smile only widened. "I actually want to laugh out loud and do a backflip. It's only out of respect for your still raging wrath on my behalf that I'm being so restrained."

He was blithely dismissing this catastrophic discovery that had shattered the very pillars of her existence.

Her crushing misery morphed into exasperation making her hiss, "This is deadly serious, Ivan."

"And I'm as deadly serious when I say I've never been this relieved. I thought I lost you and my world was ending and then you tell me this, and I'm like, 'Really? That's it? That's what she almost gave us both heart attacks over?'"

At her chagrined screech, he took both her hands, pressed kisses on them before pressing them to his heart, his gaze becoming pure persuasion. "I swear on the most precious things in my life—you and our coming child—that I really, *really* couldn't care less what your mother did. I'm not the child who went to The Organization, or the young man who escaped it, or even the man I was until I came back for you months ago. I'm now the new me, the one who loves you, the man you own. And this man has no place in his memory except for every single second since he met you, and every single second in our future together. This man is endlessly grateful that his life path—the horrific parts included—led him to you and made him into the man you love. This man cares about absolutely nothing else, as long as you love him."

His every word was a jolt supercharging her heart with a surplus of love for him that she felt she'd burst with it.

Struggling to contain it all, her hands fisted on his chest, her whole body shaking. "You can't still love me when I and my own have been the curse of your existence!"

He shook his head. "The only times I felt I was cursed was when I thought I'd lose you. And during the past three days when I thought I already had."

Feeling her head would explode with the need to get him angry, she started to protest again, but he surged, sealed her lips with his, letting her taste his life and love, his relief and delight. But it was tasting his smile that made her pull back, her blood seething.

"Ivan, you *can't*. *I* can't let you forgive. You must exact vengeance, carve out pounds of flesh, preferably from me."

He only hauled her into his arms and laid her back on the bed, enveloping her in a full body hug. "I'm taking all hundred and forty pounds of your precious, libido-igniting flesh." His eyes filled with teasing, and a trace of lingering insecurity. "That is, if you love me."

She drummed her feet on the bed in frustration. "If? It's because my whole being is ninety percent made of loving you that I'm losing my mind here."

He threw his head back and laughed, before squeezing her hard. "See this? This is exactly why I'm not only not angry with your mother I'm even glad she did what she did. It didn't only mean saving everyone, it meant saving *you*. Saving you so you'd grow up into this irreplaceable creature, so I can one day find you, and love you for the rest of my life."

Stymied beyond expression or endurance, she started weeping again. "Ivan, oh, God, Ivan, you're too much…and I love you too much, it hurts. It's *excruciating* when I think—"

"Then don't think. Or think only of this. That if I'd known the real price of my family's salvation, and yours, I *would* have paid it willingly then. I would do anything at all for you now. And knowing that, do you think I'll do nothing while you feel this horribly? Do you think I can rest while you break your own heart, and hate your mother to avenge me?"

"But I can't just forget, Ivan. I can't forgive her."

"But I want you to. Your mother did a terrible thing, at terrible times, and she's been punishing herself, eaten by guilt ever since. She has made up in every way possible for my family, and for yours. And she not only lost Alex, she feels it's her fault. That is far more punishment that any mother should have to endure, no matter her crimes. Have mercy, *moya dusha*. Forgive her here…" He pressed his open palm to her heart, making her sob and burrow into his hardness and heat. "Pity her. And most of all, love her again. I need you to. I don't want any anger or disappointment or bitterness to eat at the magnificent light and beauty inside you."

Her tears stopped. There *was* such a thing as being moved beyond tears.

His smile became crooked. "I am being partially selfish here, since I'm the primary beneficiary of your light and beauty, the one who has the most to gain from it in the form of endless pleasure and fathom-less love."

She rose to look down on him, everything inside her capitulating. Loving him beyond endurance, she whispered, "You miracle of a man who loves me be-yond my wildest imaginings no matter what. You avenging angel who will avenge anyone but yourself. Will you take me as your wife, Ivan? Will you let me have and hold you, love and cherish you, support and defend you, lose my mind over you and give my very soul to you, so that not even death will us part?"

He held her eyes in utmost solemnity. "I do."

Before she could kiss him, he beat her to it. In sec-onds he had her arching beneath him, begging for his invasion. But he pulled back, poignancy and teasing a heady mixture in his eyes. "So when will you offi-cially make an honest man out of me?"

And she did something an hour ago she'd thought she'd never do again. She giggled.

He really was a miracle. And a miracle worker.

Raining kisses on every part of him she could reach, she said, "As soon as you can get your scat-tered troops to regroup."

As if he'd been coiled and waiting to launch into action, he sprang up, got out his phone, started bark-ing orders for everyone to fall back into formation.

Half an hour later, he looked down at her in tri-umph. "As per your command, *moya dusha*, to-morrow you become Dr. Anastasia Konstantinov."

Pulling him down over her, loving him fiercely,

endlessly, she sighed into his lips. "Tomorrow, and forever."

Before he claimed her, took them both back from the brush with devastation to their exclusive heaven, he pledged, "At least that long."

Epilogue

"Forgive yourself, Grace."

At his words, Anastasia's mother turned to Ivan with a gasp.

She'd been subdued all through the wedding ceremony, and now during the reception she'd walked into a corner as if she wanted to disappear. Everyone thought her state was recurrent desolation over Alex's loss, and Ivan and Anastasia let everyone believe that. The secret of what she'd done would never get outside the four who knew it.

"I forgive you," he said. "And I do thank you for saving my family, for saving yours. But mostly for saving Anastasia. I would have forgiven you had you cost me all my limbs for this alone." As the woman's eyes filled, he persisted. "And I also want you to believe that Alex's death wasn't punishment for you, or else fate must have seen fit to punish me and everyone who loved him, too, since his death hurt us all irrevocably."

As her tears fell, he reached for her arm, gave it a gentle squeeze. And she crumpled against him, too weak to do anything but accept his absolution, letting him take her in his embrace.

He pressed a kiss to her forehead, this woman who'd once been a second mother to him, the mother of the love of his life, the reason for everything he was and did.

"People in sweeping upheavals and grave dangers make terrible decisions. But whatever your sins against me, just that you've saved Anastasia, so I could find her so many years later, love her, live for her, evens the scales and way more. Anastasia loves you. It's why she was so hurt. But I promise I'll do everything to heal her so she will open up to you again. It's what Alex would have wanted. For us all to be happy, to honor his memory. And in his memory, there will be no more losses and injuries. Never on my account, or on my watch."

A choking sound made him turn around. And there she was, Anastasia, his bride, looking far better than his wildest fantasies. She was his reward from fate, with every blessing the world had to offer in her eyes.

They'd exchanged vows an hour ago, were now husband and wife. One. At last and forever.

He extended a hand to her, and she took it at once, let him reel her in so she faced her mother.

He pressed a cherishing kiss against her flushed cheek, murmured his love and encouragement. Returning the kiss, her eyes filling with that gratitude he'd yet to make her stop feeling, she turned to her mother.

"We'll be all right, Mom. Thanks to Ivan."

The woman reached out a hand, asking Anastasia's permission for intimacy. His palm caressed Anastasia's back, urging her to take her mother's hand. As soon as she did, the woman pulled her into a brief, though fervent hug.

Then, as if she didn't want to push her luck further, with tears running down her face, Grace turned and rushed away.

After watching her mother's departure, Anastasia turned to Ivan, face brightening, eyes igniting.

Before he could scoop her to his heart again, a big hand slapped him hard on the back. *Dammit.*

"So tell me, Wildcard, how do you feel now you're a married man?"

He turned to Antonio, who was grinning at him wickedly, everything right with his world again now that he'd gotten his Liliana to forgive, *and* marry him, too. Something Ivan had had a hand in.

While he'd been with Anastasia in Russia, Antonio had called him in a bleak state, asked him to come take what amounted to his last will and testament, to give to Liliana after he'd left, ostensibly to commit accidental suicide on some frontline. Ivan had rushed to his side, then to Liliana's to make her stop him. Which she had.

Ivan had rushed back to Anastasia the next day. She'd still been sleeping so long in those days he doubted she'd even noticed he'd been away.

But when Antonio's wedding had come just a week later, he'd begged off being his best man. Anastasia hadn't been up to attending weddings at the time, and he couldn't have left her. And he couldn't bear seeing his best friend get the love of his life, when he'd felt he'd eventually lose his.

Did that make him a terrible friend? Yeah. Probably.

Antonio sure would never let him live it down.

Pulling Anastasia into his side lovingly, he crooked an eyebrow at his best friend. "Why don't you tell me first? You're an old married man now, while I'm fresh off the altar."

Antonio looked down at his wife of only two months, going positively goo-goo eyed. "It's simple really. I'm the happiest man in existence."

"Oh, no, you're not!" Ivan growled, actually annoyed at his friend's claim.

"Oh, yes, I am." Antonio all but stuck his tongue out at him.

"It's my wedding, and if I say you're not, you're not!"

The two women looked at each other…then burst out laughing.

As he and Antonio turned to their wives, demanding in mock severity what they found so funny, the rest of the gang, as Anastasia called them, converged on them.

"So what are you ladies busting a stitch over?" That was Isabella, sauntering over with that serpent husband of hers slithering right behind her. Yeah, Ivan still wasn't a fan of Richard Graves, a.k.a. Cobra. Neither was Richard a fan of his. They were both perfectly fine with this.

"Yeah, we want in on the belly laughs," said Scarlett, Raiden's wife.

Anastasia and Liliana turned to the ladies, laughing harder than ever.

"There's just something hilarious about watching these two Olympians bickering," Anastasia spluttered.

Liliana hooted in laughter. "And not any bickering. The twelve-year-old variety. Time stopped for them the day they met, it seems."

"No, it didn't," Ivan growled. "And we don't bicker!"

"You tell them, brother." Antonio squared off beside him, as always joining with him against any others.

"Oh, you bicker. You're experts at it." Eliana, Rafael's wife, gave Antonio an affectionate nudge. "Just admit it."

"It goes beyond expertise. It's a matter of survival for you boys. I don't think you can live without plucking at each other's shiny feathers." That was Jenan, Numair's wife, who'd become the leader of the gang of wives, just like Numair had been and remained their brotherhood's leader. "So what was the subject of the squabble this time?"

Anastasia feigned a shudder. "I'm afraid if we tell

you, we'd have a full-scale war among all of you on our hands."

Liliana nodded in mock trepidation. "Yes, we shouldn't say. To preserve the peace within the brotherhood."

It was the men who now spoke up, each demanding in his own inimitable way to know what the Bones/Wildcard duet had been saying behind their backs that they should be punished for.

Anastasia and Liliana finally pretended to break down under duress and divulged the sensitive subject of the debate.

As expected, each man protested, claiming the title of Happiest Man In Existence for himself, each ready to duel for it. Finally the bickering escalated to jabs and shoves, among the raucous laughter of their delighted and adoring wives.

Suddenly, all the men froze. As did Ivan.

It took the women moments to realize that the men weren't playing a collective joke on them, when they all rushed to get out their phones.

Ivan's heart hammered so hard he jumbled his password to open the screen twice. He had the same difficulty in bringing up the latest message.

After reading it, he bit his lip, for fleeting moments wondering if this was some kind of prank, wishing it was. And knowing it couldn't be.

Then he raised his gaze to his brothers, saw confirmation of that in their solemn eyes.

This was no prank. It was really him.

Cypher.

Their Black Castle brotherhood's long-lost brother.

He was texting them on the line that not even their wives had access to. With a message made of only five words.

Expect a visit...soon. Cypher.

Many hours later, the reception was over and the impromptu meeting he'd had with his brothers had revealed no insights into Cypher's message, or any projections about future developments.

Head filled with nebulous worries, Ivan now walked into their bedroom suite with Anastasia in his arms and clinging around his neck.

As he lowered her down on their bed. But as he came down half over her, started kissing her, she stopped him. And he knew why.

He'd previously explained who Cypher was, leaving out as much as he could. Which clearly hadn't satisfied her. She had more questions. Ones he didn't know if he ever could, or should, answer.

"Have any of you texted Cypher back?" she asked.

"If we could have we would. Cypher is the only one in our brotherhood who's my equal in cyber powers. He hid from even me all these years. I have no idea where he's been, what he's been doing. Or even who he is anymore."

"You all looked so...shaken at his message."

"We hadn't expected to hear from him after all these years."

"You said it didn't end well between you. All of you?"

"Yes." He *hated* talking about this, would rather be extracting molars without anesthesia. Before Anastasia could hit him with another question he only had to evade, he stretched her arms above her head. "Now enough of this. Let me make love to my bride."

And for a very long time, he did just that.

After he'd drowned them both in the ecstasy of their unity twice, Anastasia stirred in his arms.

He was savoring the drugged cast in her eyes and his own satisfaction when her question hit him out of left field. Damn. He'd managed to forget everything that existed outside of this room. Until now.

"Does this visit Cypher said to expect worry you?"

He rose above her, smiled reassuringly, and told her his very first, and what he intended to be his very last, barefaced lie.

"Of course not."

* * * * *

COMING NEXT MONTH FROM

HARLEQUIN *Desire*

Available December 6, 2016

#2485 THE BABY PROPOSAL
Billionaires and Babies • by Andrea Laurence
Lana will do anything to gain custody of her infant niece—even marry her best friend, Kal, in name only. But playing house in Kal's mansion has them both wanting to be much more than friends...

#2486 THE TEXAN'S ONE-NIGHT STANDOFF
Dynasties: The Newports • by Charlene Sands
Brooks Newport's scorching one-night stand with Ruby Lopez was unforgettable—and he wants more! Until a reunion with his long-lost father reveals Ruby to be an honorary member of the family...and completely off-limits.

#2487 MAID UNDER THE MISTLETOE
by Maureen Child
After a tragic past, millionaire Sam Henry enjoys being alone, especially for Christmas. But will his temporary holiday housekeeper's sexy smiles and enticing touch lure him back into the world—and tempt him to take a second chance on love?

#2488 THE PREGNANCY PROJECT
Love and Lipstick • by Kat Cantrell
Dante has made a fortune as Dr. Sexy. So he knows attraction when he feels it—even when the temptation is his pregnant best friend who's sworn off men! Now this expert at seduction must prove his theories work—while holding on to his heart.

#2489 RICH RANCHER FOR CHRISTMAS
The Beaumont Heirs • by Sarah M. Anderson
CJ Wesley is a Beaumont heir, and that's a secret he won't share. Especially not with a sexy-as-sin city girl looking for her next big story. But when a snowstorm strands these opposites on his ranch, their white-hot attraction proves impossible to resist!

#2490 MARRIED TO THE MAVERICK MILLIONAIRE
From Mavericks to Married • by Joss Wood
Millionaire hockey star Quinn agrees to a marriage of convenience to avoid scandal and save the biggest deal of his career. But an unplanned kiss at a masked ball ignites a fiery attraction to his new wife he can't ignore...

HDCNM1116

SPECIAL EXCERPT FROM

HARLEQUIN

Desire

*Lana will do anything to gain custody of her infant
niece—even marry her best friend, Kal, in name only.
But playing house in Kal's mansion has them both
wanting to be much more than friends...*

*Read on for a sneak peek at
THE BABY PROPOSAL,
Andrea Laurence's latest in the bestselling
BILLIONAIRES AND BABIES series!*

"What about moving in with me?"

Lana looked at him, narrowing her eyes. "That would
help a lot, actually. Are you sure, though? It's going to be
a major cramp on your bachelorhood to have me and a
baby in the house."

Kal shrugged that off. He rarely had time for anything
aside from work this time of year. Plus, if Lana was in the
house with the baby, he wouldn't miss out on his time with
her. He'd never admit to his selfish motivations, however.
"I've got three extra bedrooms just sitting empty. If it will
help, I'm happy to do what I can."

Lana beamed at him. "I'm actually really glad you
said that, because I was just about to get to the crazy part
of my plan."

Kal swallowed hard. She had something in mind that
was crazier than moving in together with a baby?

Just then Lana slid off her chair and onto one knee in

front of him. She took his hand and held it as he frowned down at her. "What are you doing?" he asked as his chest grew tight and he struggled to breathe. His hand was suddenly burning up where she held it in hers, the contact lighting his every nerve on fire. He wanted to pull away and regain control of himself, but he knew he couldn't. This was just the calm before the storm.

Lana took a deep breath and looked up at him with a hopeful smile. "I'm asking you to marry me."

Don't miss
THE BABY PROPOSAL
by Andrea Laurence,
available December 2016 wherever
Harlequin® Desire books and ebooks are sold.

www.Harlequin.com

Whatever You're Into... Passionate Reads

Looking for more passionate reads from Harlequin®?
Fear not! Harlequin® Presents, Harlequin® Desire and
Harlequin® Blaze offer you irresistible romance stories
featuring powerful heroes.

⬥HARLEQUIN *Presents*

Do you want alpha males, decadent glamour and jet-set
lifestyles? Step into the sensational, sophisticated world of
Harlequin® Presents, where sinfully tempting heroes ignite a
fierce and wickedly irresistible passion!

⬥HARLEQUIN *Desire*

Harlequin® Desire novels are powerful, passionate and
provocative contemporary romances set against a backdrop of
wealth, privilege and sweeping family saga. Alpha heroes with
a soft side meet strong-willed but vulnerable heroines amid a
dramatic world of divided loyalties, high-stakes conflict and
intense emotion.

⬥HARLEQUIN *Blaze*

Harlequin® Blaze stories sizzle with strong heroines and
irresistible heroes playing the game of modern love and lust.
They're fun, sexy and always steamy.

Be sure to check out our full selection of books
within each series every month!

www.Harlequin.com

Turn your love of reading into rewards you'll love with
Harlequin My Rewards

Join for FREE today at www.HarlequinMyRewards.com

Earn **FREE BOOKS** of your choice.

Experience **EXCLUSIVE OFFERS** and contests.

Enjoy **BOOK RECOMMENDATIONS** selected just for you.

PLUS! Sign up now and get **500** points right away!

Earn **FREE** REWARDS HarlequinMyRewards.com Join Today!

MYR16R